Belle Marshall Locke

Breezy Point

A Comedy in Three Acts

Belle Marshall Locke

Breezy Point
A Comedy in Three Acts

ISBN/EAN: 9783741187490

Manufactured in Europe, USA, Canada, Australia, Japa

Cover: Foto ©Andreas Hilbeck / pixelio.de

Manufactured and distributed by brebook publishing software
(www.brebook.com)

Belle Marshall Locke

Breezy Point

A COMEDY IN THREE ACTS

FOR FEMALE CHARACTERS ONLY

BY

BELLE MARSHALL LOCKE

AUTHOR OF "MARIE'S SECRET," "THE GREAT CATASTROPHE," ETC.

PROPERTIES.

ACT I.—Flowers for Elinor and Ashrael, newspapers on table, travelling-bags for girls, letter for Ashrael, dinner-bell ready off left.

ACT II.—Pan of water, dish-cloth and dishes for Ashrael, dish-towel for Fantine, camera for Bernice, drawing-portfolio for Clarice, two tin pails for the twins, bag of candy for Laura, work basket with stockings for Aunt Debby, pan of pop-corn for Elinor, carpet-bag, small satchel, band-box and umbrella for Miss Doolittle, glass of lemonade for Elinor, book for Ashrael, dinner-horn for Elinor, pan of apples and knife for Aunt Debby, basin of water, sponge and bandages for Elinor, baskets for Old Clem, glass of wine and crackers for Aunt Debby, tomato can for Laura, letter and valise for Fantine, large basket for Elinor, fan for Clarice.

ACT III.—Camera for Bernice, small tin box for Miss Doolittle, basket and packages for Ashrael, letter for Edith, satchel and box of roses for Aunt Debby, glass of wine for Ashrael.

BREEZY POINT.

ACT I.

SCENE.—*Sitting-room at Breezy Point. Table* R., *with books, newspapers, etc. Chairs each side, with hassock* L. *Couch* L. *Small table, with lamp, at head of couch. Easy-chair by table. Bookcase up* L. *Easel, with picture, up* R. *Door, with portières* C. ELINOR *at table* R., ASHRAEL, L. *of table, discovered, arranging flowers.*

ELINOR. There, Ashrael! (*Holding up bouquet.*) This will do for the front chamber. You say that you have filled the vases for the other rooms?

ASHRAEL. Yes, Miss Elinor, I've put narsturtimums in the room at the head of the stairs, sweet peas in the corner room, an' a mixter in the back chamber.

ELINOR. A what?

ASHRAEL. A mixter. Bein' as you're goin' to put that fur-rin maid in that room, I thought a mixed bokay would be more 'propriate for her.

ELINOR (*laughing*). You always had a nice sense of the fitness of things, Ashrael.

ASHRAEL. Yes, I'm might pertickler about things fittin'; an' speakin' of that makes me think, my red bask, that Miss Cuttin' made, fits like all possessed. I can turn 'round twice in it; an' there ain't much chance of fattin' up, bein' as you're goin' to have a house full of summer boarders, every one of 'em high-falutin' girls, who'll want some one to dance attendance on 'em from mornin' till night.

ELINOR. Bring your waist to me to-night, after supper, Ashrael, and I'll fix it for you. I am sorry to hear you speak so of the young ladies who are coming to stay with us. You know, as well as I, Ashrael, that there is a heavy mortgage on Breezy Point, and if something is not done to meet the payments, dear, patient Aunt Debby will have to leave the only home she

5

ever knew. She has been so good to you and me, Ashrael,
surely we want to do what little we can to help her.

ASHRAEL (*wiping her eyes on apron*). You make me feel
meaner'n pusley, Miss Elinor. Course I wants to do all I can,
but it's in my blood to grumble, an' I can't help it to save my
life! Forgot? Well, I guess I hain't forgot how Miss Dexter
took me out of the poorhouse five years ago, and how you've
both been a-doin' for me ever sence. I'll make you proud of
me some day ; see if I don't!

ELINOR. I hope so, Ashrael.

ASHRAEL. Yes, sir-ree! I'm still aspirin', an' them work-
house imps, who used to call me " Ashes," will find there was
a spark left in 'em, that'll make a blaze one of these days.
There, these are all ready now an' I'll jest have time to put 'em
on the bureaus an' sweep the front piazza, before the train comes
with that tribe of pesky—(*rises*) er—with the young ladies.
(*Aside.*) My tongue gets longer an' sharper every day !
[*Exit* L.

ELINOR. I'm afraid that I feel something as Ashrael does
about a crowd of noisy girls invading our quiet place ; but if
my little scheme will bring some money to Aunt Debby, and
drive that careworn look from her sweet face, I'd be happy in
Bedlam.   [*Rises.*

AUNT DEBBY (*outside*). Vanilla flavoring, Bridget, don't
forget. (*Enters* L.) Ah, you are here, my dear. I'm a little
anxious about the pudding, for I'm not quite sure that Bridget
is the experienced cook she would have us think she is.

ELINOR. Sit down a few minutes, Aunt Debby, and get
cool. You look a bit "flustrated," as Ashrael would say.
(AUNT DEBBY *sits* L. *of table* R., *and* ELINOR *takes rose from
table*.) Isn't that a beauty ? I saved it for you. (*Pins it on
her gown*.) We have a few moments before the train comes
and let's compose ourselves.   [*Sits on hassock at her feet.*

AUNT DEBBY. Ah, Elinor, I fear this is a wild scheme of
yours ; and now that the time draws near, I'm afraid this little
place, that is so dear to us, will be very dull to those gay school-
girls.

ELINOR. It will be perfectly delightful to them, Aunt Debby,
mark my words ! Just think what a humdrum life they must
lead at Madame Finikin's city boarding-school, and what a
delight these big meadows, the grove and the lake will be to
them !

AUNT DEBBY. Yes, I know, but——

ELINOR. "But me no buts !" Two of the girls' parents
have gone abroad and they couldn't go home ; one of them has
money enough to buy friends, to be sure, but the poor thing
hasn't a living relative in the country ; and the other can't go to

her home, because there is scarlet fever in the house. The girls wanted to be together, and when I read Madame Finikin's advertisement for a nice summer home for them, I knew Breezy Point was just the place. And then the money, Aunt Debby, just think of that! We can meet the payment on the mortgage in the fall all right.

AUNT DEBBY. What a treasure you are, Elinor, and what a comfort you have been to me all these years!

ELINOR. Sent to you market-fashion, Aunt Debby. I've pictured you many times finding me a little baby in a basket, at your door. Why, didn't you send me to the poorhouse?

AUNT DEBBY. Because, dear, when I pulled the blanket aside, you raised your tiny arms to me and smiled; and from that moment, even before I lifted you from your rough nest, you had crept into my heart and I loved you.

ELINOR. I know it, Aunt Debby, I am sure of it, for I have never felt the loss of a mother's love, only——

AUNT DEBBY. Only you want to know who that mother was, dear, I understand; but there was no mark but the name Elinor on your blanket. Then I called you Elinor Pearl, because you are the little pearl I found! There was nothing to serve as a clue; but you came from no poor place, Elinor, for your clothing was of the richest, finest quality.

ELINOR. Ah, why—— [*Rises.*

AUNT DEBBY. There, there, child, dismiss it from your mind. Eighteen years have gone since then, but some day I feel that the mystery will be cleared, and in the meantime you have me, my dear.

ELINOR (*throwing arms about her neck*). Yes, I have you! and I ought to be the happiest girl——

ASHRAEL (*showing girls in* C.). Right this way. They've come, Miss Dexter.

[*Bus. for* ASHRAEL *examining girls curiously, tossing head at French maid, etc.*

BERNICE. This is Miss Dexter, I presume. I am Bernice Vernon, and these young ladies are Clarice Fenleigh, Edith Norton and Laura Leigh.

[AUNT DEBBY *shakes hands with all of the girls as they are introduced.*

AUNT DEBBY. You are welcome to Breezy Point, and I hope you will be happy with us. This is my niece Elinor Pearl, and I am sure she joins me in bidding you welcome.

ELINOR. Indeed I do! and I hope you will like this place one-half as well as we do.

BERNICE. I am sure we shall like it.

EDITH. We have been in ecstasies over the scenery all the way from the station.

AUNT DEBBY. And now, as you must be tired after your journey, you will want to go to your rooms at once. Ashrael, show the young ladies upstairs.

BERNICE (*as the girls are going out*). This is my maid, Miss Dexter. I hope it has not been too much trouble for you to accommodate her.

AUNT DEBBY. None at all, my dear, we have plenty of room. (ASHRAEL *shows them out* L.) A bright, pretty lot of girls, Elinor ! Maybe it won't be so bad after all.

ELINOR. Of course it won't, Aunt Debby. You will be in love with every one of them before a week is over. (*Laughing.*) Oh, I know your soft heart !

AUNT DEBBY. At any rate, you occupy the softest place in it, my dear.

ELINOR. And I'm going to try and keep it, I give you fair warning ! But tell me, what can I do to help you ?

AUNT DEBBY. Not a thing, only look after those girls, if they want anything. I am going to see if Bridget's getting on all right with the dinner, for I know they must be hungry.

[*Exit* L.

ELINOR (*folding newspaper, arranging table, etc.*). Dear Aunt Debby ! She is always thinking of other people, always trying to make them happy. Why, she even signed her home away to raise money to save a worthless brother from disgrace. Ah, well, he is dead and gone and so is the money, and I must try and use my wits, as well as my hands, to save this dear old place. (*Dropping into chair* L. *of table.*) What a terrible thing it is not to know your own name ! I wonder if I have a mother in this big world, and why she thrust me, a helpless child, among strangers. I look at the veins in my hands sometimes, and wonder whose blood flows in them. I look in the glass, and long to know if my face is like my mother's ; but, most of all, I want to feel that she was good and innocent ! And yet that doubt is always in my mind. (*Buries face in hands, crying.*) But I must stop thinking ! How wicked I am, and how it would grieve Aunt Debby to see me like this. (*Rises.*) I'll run up-stairs and bathe my eyes. (*Sound of girls laughing merrily.*) How happy they are, those girls ! And I'm going to be happy too ! I'm not going to play the role of " Aunty Doleful," and if I've one bit of energy in my nature it's time to assert it.

[*Exit* L., *singing,* " *It's better to laugh than be sighing.*"

Enter ASHRAEL, C.

ASHRAEL. There ! I've got 'em located, lugged up hot water enough to drown 'em, an' now I'm to wait here, ready to be at their beck an' call, (*sits by table*) an' I'm a-goin' to do it cheerful, too, 'cause I said I would. That French maid jest makes me sick ! I'll let her know she can't put upon me ! I'll try to do my level best for those girls, but that critter has jest got to keep out from under my feet ! There's one good thing about it, they all seem to like the place, an' their rooms suited 'em to a T. I couldn't help laffin' to hear 'em rave over the scenery. I never could see anything so awful wonderful about old Mt. Prospect ; 'tain't nothin' but a mountin anyway ; and Lily Lake ain't much to look at, but they nearly had highstericks over it. I heard 'em a-plannin' to climb Blueberry Hill, to-morrer, to get a view. If they'd gone up there berryin' as many times as I have, an' scratched themselves 'bout to death an' tore their clothes 'most off 'em, they wouldn't be in such a rush to try it. (*Rises.*) But that's always the way ! Folks that *has* to do things don't want to. Goodness gracious ! there's that letter I got from Billy Griffin this mornin' in my pocket now, an' I hain't had time to read it. (*Takes it out of pocket.*) Billy's well enough in his place, but I'm lookin' higher than to marry a butcher. I'm goin' to aspire as long as I live ! I don't know what it'll amount to, but I'm goin' to be somethin' ; I hain't decided what yet. (*Looks at letter.*) Dreadful queer penman, Billy is. I hope he likes his place over to Greggsville. It was an awful relief to get him out of here. (*Opens letter and reads to herself.*) Yes, same old story ! He's fairly dyin' for love of me. (*Reads.*) "I shall shoot myself before the year is out if you do not consent to be my lawful wedded wife." He got that out of a book I lent him. (*Reads.*) "My blood will be upon your head." His blood be upon my head. Well, I guess not ! What an idea ! I 'spose butchers always write kinder bloody. Goodness ! here's that French wriggler. (*Puts letter in bosom.*) She makes me think of an angle worm.

Enter FANTINE, C.

FANTINE. Oh, you are here, Ashreel.

ASHRAEL. Yes, there ain't no mistake about my bein' here! (*Sits* R. *of table.*) But Ash-reel ain't my name.

FANTINE. Oh, pardonnez moi. I thinks you said zat was your name.

ASHRAEL. No, I didn't ! I said Ash, A-s-h. You got that ?

FANTINE. Oui, Ash.

ASHRAEL. No, *we* ain't Ash, I am.

FANTINE (*laughing*). Well zen, Ash.

ASHRAEL. R-a—ra ; do, ra, like the scale, you know.

FANTINE. Ah, yes, ra.

ASHRAEL. E-l—the ell of a house, you know. Ash-ra-el !

FANTINE. Ah, I haf it now—Ash-rah-eel !

ASHRAEL. For goodness' sake, don't you know nothin'

scarcely ? It jest gives me the shivers to hear my name said wrong.

FANTINE. Ah, nevare mind such a leetle, small thing as zat ! You like zis place ?

'ASHRAEL. Like it ? Why, I'm dead stuck on it ! I got my health here.

FANTINE. You were sick ?

ASHRAEL. Well, I was boarding where there was a lot of old, helpless people, an' it kinder affected my nerves, so I came over here, an' my physician said I must help round, for my health. I needed exercise.

FANTINE. It seems vera quiet here.

ASHRAEL. Well, the band don't play every day, an' the streets ain't crowded.

FANTINE. I lofe ze town, where I can go to some dances an' meet some zhentlemens.

ASHRAEL. Do you know how to waltz ?

FANTINE. I know how to waltz ? Like a leetle fairy !

ASHRAEL. I kinder want to learn to waltz. It might come handy.

FANTINE. I shall teach you. (*Rises and goes stage centre.*) Come here, Ashrael. (ASHRAEL *on her right ;* FANTINE *raising skirt.*) Place your foot like zis. One ! (ASHRAEL *places foot awkwardly.*) Now, two ! (ASHRAEL *imitates.*) Three ! Now take your skirts like zis an' follow me. '(*Waltzing.*) 'Tis vera easy.

ASHRAEL (*gazing at her*). Well, if you think I'm going to hold my dress up like that, show my stockings an' go bobbing round like a five-cent top, you'll get left. I don't want to dance anyway ; it hain't dignified.   [*Sits at table as before.*

FANTINE. I lofe it ! (*Sits L. of table.*) Oh, Ashrael ! I breaks so many hearts. You have no—what you call the sweet-hearts, here ?

ASHRAEL. Nonsense ! the woods are full of 'em.

FANTINE. In ze woods ! What for do they go in ze woods ?

ASHRAEL. Oh, I mean there is lots of 'em. Beaux to burn ! I'm bothered to death with 'em.

FANTINE. How lofely ! You shall gif some to me.

ASHRAEL. Help yourself.

FANTINE. Tell me about zose sweethearts !

ASHRAEL. Well, as a nation, we don't brag much about our beaux. We kinder keep still about 'em.

FANTINE. And zat lettare, zat leetle billet-doux, I see you hide in your bosom, is zat from one of ze beaux ?

ASHRAEL (*aside*). I'll bet that girl has got a row of eyes all round her head ; but for the land sake, how did she know his name was Billy ?

FANTINE. You speak not, but I see ze leetle blush on your cheek! Ah, tell me about ze lettare.

ASHRAEL. Well, there ain't much to tell, (*loftily*) only the writer of it intends to shoot himself because I won't have him, that's all.

FANTINE. To shoot heemself? How gr-r-and! I should lofe to have a man shoot heemself for me.

ASHRAEL. I can't say I am fussy about it; still if he's bound to do it, I can't prevent him.

FANTINE. Ceretainly not! It would be vera nice.

ASHRAEL. There's one thing certain, I sha'n't give up aspiring an' marry a man jest to keep the breath of life in him.

FANTINE. Geeve up what?

ASHRAEL. My high-born asperations. Don't you know what them be?

FANTINE. No. Je ne comprend pas.

ASHRAEL. Oh, talk United States!

FANTINE. Pardonnez moi, I know not what you mean by asperasions.

ASHRAEL. I mean that I'm goin' to be somethin' great sometime; I don't know jest what; I ain't decided. (*Rocks violently.*) I may be an opery singer, a dancer——

FANTINE. No, no, I thinks not!

ASHRAEL. Or an actor. I can't tell.

FANTINE. Ah, you mean zat you will study to be some great artiste?

ASHRAEL. I don't know as I shall be an artist. I can't draw a barn. I might be a painter, for I painted the fence and it looked well; still I can't tell. I don't know what turn my talents will take.

FANTINE. Where is the man who, for you, will shoot heemself?

ASHRAEL. He's over to Greggsville. He's comin' over to-morrer night, an' I'll interduce you if you want to see him. He ain't much to look at, but he's deep, *awful* deep.

FANTINE. Ah, I shall be enchanted, fasceenated.

ASHRAEL. You can try all your French tricks on him that you're a min'ter; he won't even look at no girl but me. He says he's "loyal to the heart's core." I don't know how fur in that is, but I guess it's pretty fur.

FANTINE. What is he's beesness?

ASHRAEL (*rises and walks* L.). Oh—he—he—dabbles in blood, cuts and slashes, you know.

FANTINE. Ah, I see, he is a doctor.

ASHRAEL. Yes, he doctors calves, sheeps, pigs, an' the like, an' when he gets through with 'em they never have another pain.

FANTINE (*rising*).   He must be gr-r-and in hees profession
—a vet-vet-erenerery surzhon !

ASHRAEL (*aside*).   Ain't she a greenhorn !   I'll put a flea
in Billy's ear not to let on he's a butcher.   (*Aloud.*)   How long
have you been livin' without work ?

FANTINE.   What you say ?

ASHRAEL.   How long have you been a maid ?

FANTINE.   Oh, tree year ; but not with Mademoiselle Verenon only two month.   Her maid got married an' I got ze position ; but I will get married also, when ze chance to me comes.

ASHRAEL.   You'll have quite a chance to rest before it arrives,
I reckon.

BERNICE (*outside*).   Fantine ! Fantine !

FANTINE.   She is calling to me.   I will see you some more,
when it is later; Ashreel.   *[Exit* C.

ASHRAEL.   Ashreel !   That makes me fightin' mad to hear
her say it that way ; but it's no use tryin' to learn her anything,
her head's thick as a board.   Ain't she got a soft chance,
though !   Jest to comb that girl's hair, hook up her dress, an'
little jobs like that ; then she lives in the city, an' prob'ly she'll
go across the water with her this fall.   I heard 'em say something 'bout it.   I'd go with one meal a day the rest of my life,
if I could go over there !

Enter CLARICE, LAURA *and* EDITH, C.

LAURA.   What time do we dine, Ashrael ?   I believe that is
your name ?

ASHRAEL.   Yes, miss, you've got it right, for a wonder.   We
dines jest as the clock strikes one.   *[Exit* L.

LAURA.   "We" dines at one, do you hear ?   Come on, girls,
let's take a run over in the grove yonder !   Bernice is going ;
she's getting ready now.

CLARICE.   I do not think I'll go out, Laura, until after the
sun goes down.   My head is trying to ache and I'm pretty sure
it will succeed if I give it half a chance, (*sits on couch*) but you
go, Edith.

EDITH.   No, I'll stay with you.   Run along, Laura, with Bernice, and find all the pretty nooks.   We'll be with you to-mor-
row, sure.

LAURA.   All right !   Take care of your head, Clarice.

EDITH.   And don't you fail to be here at one !   I'm hungry
as a bear.

LAURA.   " There are others ! "   Don't worry ; we'll be here.
          [Exit C.

EDITH (*going back of couch and rubbing* CLARICE'S *head*).
I don't like these headaches ; they are by far too frequent.

CLARICE. Well, as a steady diet, I think, myself, they are not satisfactory.

EDITH. Why, you aren't one bit like the merry girl you were last year. I've wished a dozen times that you had gone abroad with your parents. Now, I was just crazy to go, but my folks didn't want me, and you were urged to go and wouldn't. All goes to prove that when you can have a thing, you don't want it, and when you can't you're crazy for it.

CLARICE. ·You're quite a philosopher, Edith ; but, seriously, I didn't go abroad ·because I hadn't the slightest interest in it.

EDITH (*sitting in chair* L., *near couch*). You have no interest in anything, that's the trouble. Once you used to tell me everything that worried you, and now I know that something is on your mind and you won't tell-me. ` It isn't like you, Clarice.

CLARICE. I suppose not ; nothing is like me that I say or do.

EDITH. You can't be worrying over your studies, for you are sure of graduating in a few months, and you are always at the head of your class. It isn't that you are in need of anything, for you are fairly loaded with the good things of this world. Then again it isn't that you are dissatisfied with yourself personally, for you are, most assuredly, the girl where, as Hamlet says, "every god did set his seal." It must be that you're in love, Clarice ; but why should that worry you ? You never yet smiled upon a masculine specimen that he didn't straightway become your slave.

CLARICE. I've made a fool of myself, Edith, and that's all there is about it !

EDITH. I don't believe it, Clarice, you haven't the right material and you'd spoil in the making. But now, seriously, tell me truly, dear, what ails you, (*sits on couch by* CLARICE) and maybe I'll find a way to help you. Just wait a minute. (*Curls feet under her.*) There ! Now just imagine we are in a play. The lights are down and the big fiddle goes zub, zub, zub, while you confide your secret to me. Maybe you are crossing the proverbial bridge before you come to it.

CLARICE. No, I am not ; I have got half-way over, and I can't find my way back, and I won't go on. There's very little to tell, Edith, but maybe it would relieve me to speak of it.

EDITH. I am sure it would. Go on, dear.

CLARICE. Of course you know that Charlie Grierson went away suddenly, last winter.

EDITH. What of that ? He'll come back.

CLARICE. Well, you don't know that I'd learned to care very much for him.

EDITH. No !

CLARICE. Yes ; and matters had gone so far that he had asked me to marry him.

EDITH. Oh, Clara! And you?

CLARICE. It was the night before our reception that he told me how—how much he cared for me, and I answered that I would give him his reply the next night, at the party.

EDITH. Yes, go on!

CLARICE. Well, the next day I got a dear little note from him, asking me to wear the flowers that he sent, if I wished to make him happy. Well, the box was filled with violets—beautiful English violets. I was so happy, dear, when I pinned them in my belt. I wore a bunch in my hair, too.

EDITH. I remember. They were lovely and so were you.

CLARICE. I had scarcely entered the hall when I saw him. He started toward me, then turned, like a flash, and left the room. I have never seen or heard one word from him since. I only learned that he had gone away.

EDITH. Oh, Clarice! it was——

CLARICE. It was shameful! and I'll never get over it.

EDITH. There must have been some mistake.

CLARICE. How could there have been? I had his note and the flowers, and I wore them at his request. . He just made me show my heart and laughed at me for it! I hate——

EDITH. No, you don't, dear, you know——

Enter ELINOR, L., *pulling* AUNT DEBBY *after her.*

ELINOR (*laughing*). Come along! I sha'n't let you go. You've got to rest, until Ashrael rings the dinner-bell. Everything is all right and—— (*Discovers girls.*) Oh, I didn't know you were here. I thought you had gone out.

EDITH (*rising*). Bernice and Laura have gone, but I stayed in with Clarice. She has a headache.

AUNT DEBBY (*sitting at small table* L.). Oh, that's too bad! But don't you worry, dear, our mountain air will cure all your aches and pains.

ELINOR (*laughing*). If it doesn't, Aunt Debby will dose you with herb tea, until you will get well in self-defence.

AUNT DEBBY. Now, Elinor! that's hardly fair. I am sure——

ASHRAEL (*looking in* C.). Yes, she's here. You can walk right in, Mis' Hardscratch. Miss Dexter, here's some one to see you. [*Shows* MRS. HARDSCRATCH *in and exit.*

AUNT DEBBY (*rising*). How do you do, Mrs. Hardscratch? Come in. You look tired and warm.

[*She gives her the chair from which she has risen.* AUNT DEBBY *sits* L. *of table* R., ELINOR R. *of it*, EDITH *on arm of couch near* CLARICE.

MRS. HARDSCRATCH. Yes, it's awful hot in the sun, an' I've

been berryin' over on Blueberry Hill. I thought you might want the berries, bein' as you've got a house full of folks, so I stopped here instid of cartin 'em home.

AUNT DEBBY. Why, yes, I shall be very glad of them. Elinor, introduce the girls.

ELINOR (*rising*). Mrs. Hardscratch, these are the young ladies who are going to stay with us a while, Miss Fenleigh and Miss Norton.

MRS. HARDSCRATCH (*rising and shaking hands with girls*). I'm glad to see you well. (*To* AUNT DEBBY.) Are these all there is of 'em?

EDITH (*laughing*). No, Mrs. Hardscratch, there are more of us, but they aren't in. (*Aside, to* CLARICE.) Isn't she a specimen!

AUNT DEBBY. How many berries did you bring us, Mrs. Hardscratch?

MRS. HARDSCRATCH. Four quarts good an' heapin'. I hid 'em out under the stairs, as there's no trustin' hired help, nor no one else, for that matter.

CLARICE. I'm afraid you're a pessimist, Mrs. Hardscratch.

MRS. HARDSCRATCH. No, I'm a Baptist, Free-will. Before we moved from the old Bill Smith place up to the farm, the deacon kept store: an' I tell you 'twas a sight to see a lot of men set 'round the store evenin's an' eat raisins, crackers, apples, anything they could lay hold of! I soon cured 'em of it, though, for I soaked the crackers in kerosene, covered the raisins with cayenne pepper, an' set the apples where they couldn't get at 'em.

ELINOR (*laughing*). No one but you, Mrs. Hardscratch, would have thought of it.

MRS. HARDSCRATCH. Well, when you have to think for two it will sharpen your wits.

EDITH. For two?

MRS. HARDSCRATCH. Yes, the deacon never had the headache from thinking too much, an' then he's so mealy-mouthed, he darsn't say his soul's his own. I knew it when I married him, an' if I hadn't felt sure of myself, I should never have undertaken the job.

CLARICE. Then you believe in the subjugation of man, Mrs. Hardscratch?

MRS. HARDSCRATCH. No, I don't exactly believe they came from monkeys, but I do believe you ought to keep 'em where they belong! Give 'em an inch an' they'll take an ell. The deacon's little, but he's got the temper of a meat-axe.

ELINOR. Why, I should never have suspected it. He looks the mildest of men.

MRS. HARDSCRATCH. Well, he'd ought to; he's had twenty-five years' trainin'. I made up my mind, years ago, that if any

one was goin' to look meek, I'd ruther it would be him than me.
It all depends on the way you begin.

EDITH (*to* CLARICE).   Listen and be wise !

CLARICE.   Poor man !—poor Deacon Hardscratch !

MRS. HARDSCRATCH (*to* CLARICE).   'Pears to me you don't
look very well.   Kinder pindlin', aint' you ?

CLARICE.   I am usually very well, Mrs. Hardscratch, but I
have a headache to-day, that's all.

MRS. HARDSCRATCH.   All ?   I should think that was enough!
Why, I had two sisters, a cousin and an aunt die of headaches.
I didn't know but what they would go through the whole family ;
so I says to myself, "Somethin's got to be done to cure 'em, or
there won't be none of us left to tell the tale."   So I jest set to
work an' made some medicine that'll cure headaches every
time.   It'll only cost you a dollar a bottle.   Sha'n't I send you
over a bottle ?

CLARICE.   Thank you, Mrs. Hardscratch, I do not think I
need medicine.   I expect this air will make me quite strong, so
you needn't trouble——

MRS. HARDSCRATCH.   No- trouble at all.   I'll send the
deacon over with it to-night, on his way to meetin'.

EDITH (*aside to* CLARICE).   You're in for it !

CLARICE.   Did you ever hear anything like that ?

MRS. HARDSCRATCH.   Now that I'm here, Miss Dexter, I
might as well ask you if you don't want some eggs.   The hens
are layin' like fury now.

AUNT DEBBY.   Well, maybe——

MRS. HARDSCRATCH.   Oh, you'll need 'em, for city folks are
great feeders.   I had some at our house one year, and it seemed
to me I should never fill 'em up.

AUNT DEBBY.   We only hope they will like our country fare.

MRS. HARDSCRATCH.   Don't worry, they'll eat anything you
set before 'em.   Well, (*rising*) I s'pose I might as well be goin .

AUNT DEBBY.   Won't you stay and have some dinner, Mrs.
Hardscratch ?

MRS. HARDSCRATCH.   Thank you, I don't care if I do, bein'
as I'm here.   The deacon took his dinner into the field, and the
twins know where the vittles is, so they can hustle for themselves ; so I guess, if you'll excuse me, I'll jest slip out to the
sink an' wash my hands.   [*Exit* L.

ELINOR.   Oh, Aunt Debby, how could you ask her to
dinner !

AUNT DEBBY.   Why, my dear, I couldn't be rude.

EDITH (*to* CLARICE).   Just watch me eat !   I'll shock her.

Enter BERNICE, LAURA *and* OLD CLEM, *a gipsy*, C.

BERNICE.   We met this old gipsy woman down the road and

she says she tells fortunes. We didn't want Claire or Edith to miss having their fate revealed, so we asked her up to the house.

LAURA. Do you mind, Miss Dexter?

AUNT DEBBY. Not at all, my dear. This is Old Clem; she is no stranger to us.

CLEM. I can tell the pretty ladies something they would like to know.

ELINOR. Yes, indeed, Clem is an old acquaintance. She has been here every summer for years; but I haven't seen you for a long while, Clem. Why haven't you been up to Breezy Point?

CLEM. A snake bit my foot and I've been lame.

ELINOR. A snake?

CLEM. Well, you folks call it rheumatiz.

EDITH. Don't you get very tired of camp life?

CLEM (C.). No, I love it! I hate the houses! I should suffocate under a roof. Shall I tell your fortune, lady? Cross the poor old gipsy's hand with silver.

[ASHRAEL *ringing dinner-bell.*

ELINOR. There's the dinner-bell. I'm afraid you won't have time to have your fortunes told now, girls. Why can't we go down to the camp to-night?

BERNICE. Oh, yes, that would be much better.

AUNT DEBBY (*at door* L.). Dinner is ready; right this way, please.

BERNICE (*to* ELINOR, *as they go out*). You tell her to expect us after supper. [*Exit girls*, L.

ELINOR. You heard me promise to take the girls down to-night, didn't you, Clem?

CLEM. Yes, I heard.

ELINOR. And I'll bring you a basket of food and a bottle of currant wine.

CLEM. Bless your bright eyes!

ELINOR. And you'll tell my fortune, too, this time, won't you? You know I've often coaxed you.

CLEM. No! but I'll tell theirs, good or bad. I'll take *their* money. I hate their high an' haughty ways, curse 'em! I hate 'em root an' branch! [*Up* C.

ELINOR (*up* L. *hands to ears*). Oh, don't, Clem!

CLEM (*patting her head*). There, there, I didn't mean to hurt your pretty ears.

ELINOR. You *will* tell my fortune to-night, won't you?

CLEM. No, I tell you! You're better off not to hear it, better off! [*Exit* C. ELINOR *looking after her.*

CURTAIN.

2

ACT II.

SCENE.—*A camp in the woods. Six weeks later. Kitchen table up* R. C. *If convenient, a tent should be used up* R., *the entrance visible. A couple of rustic benches, chairs and camp-stools scattered about stage.* ASHRAEL *discovered at table, washing dishes.* FANTINE *on her right, wiping them.*

FANTINE. This is not ze work I was to do when Mademoiselle Verenon asks of me to be her maid !

ASHRAEL. 'Twon't hurt you I reckon. Folks can't camp out, unless some one does the work, an' you was tickled as could be when you found out we was goin' to live a spell out doors.

FANTINE. I thought me it would be vera romantic ; but the flies do bite me and the sun does spoil my face.

ASHRAEL. I reckon they won't eat you ! You'll have face enough left, don't worry ? Where did you sneak to last night, after dark ? I couldn't find you nowhere.

FANTINE. I heard somebody's call, in a vera queer voice, to whip a boy, by the name of Will, and I went to find him.

ASHRAEL. Well, greenie, that was a bird. Night before last I hunted for you, an' you's nowhere to be found. You're as slippery as an eel.

FANTINE. I went to look at ze moon.

ASHRAEL. Because there was a man it it, I suppose. You must have liked the looks of him', cause you's gone two hours. I jest thought you'd gone down to the village to see that feller that works in Brown's grocery store. You've been cuttin' up like sixty sence I interdooced you to a few fellers. You act as though you never saw one before, an' you was afraid some of 'em would get away ; but you've found one that don't run after you, an' that's Billy Griffin.

FANTINE. Billee is vera quiet.

ASHRAEL. 'Course he is ! When a feller's been in love five years, an' hain't got no encouragement, he ain't apt to be very frisky. There ! them dishes are done now, thank goodness ; an' I'm goin' to lay down, under some tree, an' read " The Pirate's Bride." I left her hangin' over a precipice, an' he was runnin' might an' main, to save her.

FANTINE. Oh, read zat to me, Ashreel !

ASHRAEL. Come along. I'll make your eyes stick out, an' give you the shivers so you won't sleep for a week.

[ASHRAEL *and* FANTINE *exeunt* L.

Enter LAURA, BERNICE *and* EDITH, R.

LAURA (*laughing*). I tell you, Edith, it's a sight to see the
way Bernice chases folks with her camera !

[EDITH *on camp-stool* L., LAURA *and* BERNICE *on
rustic bench* R.

BERNICE. Well, didn't I get some beauties, this morning ?

LAURA. Yes, she even went down to the blacksmith's and
caught him shoeing a horse. But where is Clarice ?

EDITH. Oh, she's been gone all the morning, sketching an
old mill that she discovered last week. Elinor went with her.
I say, isn't she the dearest girl, you ever saw ?

LAURA. Who ?

EDITH. Why, Elinor, of course.

BERNICE. Yes, she makes me ashamed of myself every hour
in the day, she is so unselfish. I wish I could do something for
her ; but goodness ! she's so proud about anything like that, I
wouldn't dare mention it.

EDITH. I'd give a good deal if I could sing as she can !

BERNICE. She has a marvellous voice, and here I am, with
just an ordinary, every day kind of a voice, going abroad this
fall to study.

LAURA. Don't underrate yourself, Miss ! You know that you
sing like a nightingale.

EDITH. Bernice knows it.

BERNICE. I do not. I know that I've studied for three years
and there isn't one-half the melody in my voice that Elinor has
in hers ; and here I am, without a relative, throwing money
away on myself all of the time, when I'd be so happy to give that
girl a chance to study.

EDITH. You have such a big heart that you may find it
troublesome, one of these days, Bernice.

BERNICE. Never fear ! My heart is engaged to Mr. Am-
bition and they are going to live in peace and unity.

EDITH. And Laura's parents have really consented to
allow her to go abroad with you ?

BERNICE. Yes, and I am going to dose that lazy girl with
enthusiasm three times a day before meals, as the prescriptions
read, and you may expect to hear a violiniste, when she comes
back, who will make you all proud to say : "Ah, yes, I went to
school with her at Madame Finikin's !"

LAURA (*rising*). Do keep still, Bernice ! I sha'n't amount to
a row of pins, I know I never shall. But here are the truants,
chattering like magpies.

Enter CLARICE *and* ELINOR, R.

CLARICE. Ah, girls, we've had the greatest time ! Rode on
a load of hay !

EDITH.   Oh, dear ! and I missed it.

CLARICE.   I should say so !   You see I had sketched the mill all right and we were coming back to camp by the road, when we met— who was it, Elinor ?

ELINOR.   Mr. Drake with a load of hay.

CLARICE.   And who do you think was with him, Edith ?

EDITH.   His freckled hired hand, I suppose.

CLARICE.   No, Miss.   Dick Coleman, who was sweet on you last year.

EDITH.   Dick here ?   I thought he was in the Adirondacks ! Where is he staying ?   Did he know I was here ?   Shall we see him ?

CLARICE.   One at a time, please.

LAURA.   Edith is just like a phonograph ; when she gets wound up, she just——

EDITH.   Do keep still ! Clarice, why don't you tell me ? You're the most provoking girl ! Elinor, you answer me.

ELINOR.   Well, Dick, as you call him, is here, surely, and——

CLARICE.   Let me answer every other question.   He has been in the Adirondacks, but some magnet drew him up among these hills.   Go on, Elinor, it's your inning.

ELINOR.   And he's staying at Mr. Drake's, two miles from here.

CLARICE.   And he asked for you.

ELINOR.   And he's coming to take you for a drive, later.

EDITH.   How perfectly lovely !

BERNICE.   I never saw such a little goose, Edith !

EDITH.   Oh, you can just go and split your throat singing, but I'd rather hear Dick whisper three words, than all the Italian things you can learn in a year.

LAURA.   There's honesty for you !

AUNT DEBBY (*appearing* R.).   Girls we are out of milk. Some one must go over to Mrs. Hardscratch's and get some.

BERNICE.   Come, Laura, we will go.   Clarice and Elinor are tired, and Edith wouldn't know if she were sent for milk, or cheese.   (*Looking off* R.)   But who is coming down the path ?   I do believe they are the Hardscratch twins, for they are as alike as two peas.

ELINOR (*looking*).   Yes, here are the twins, spick span clean, in their new aprons.

Enter BETHIA *and* SOPHIA HARDSCRATCH,
with can and tin-pail, R.

ELINOR.   Halloo, girls ! what have you brought us ?

BETHIA.   Some milk.

SOPHIA. Yes, milk.

BERNICE. We were just going over to your house for some and you've saved us a long walk.

ELINOR. But what's in the pail ? [*Takes pail and can.*

BETHIA. Butter.

SOPHIA. Jest butter. [ELINOR *exit* R.

LAURA. Sit down ; you look tired.

BETHIA. It's awful hot !

SOPHIA. Awful ! [*They sit* R.

EDITH. And echo answers——

CLARICE. Keep still, Edith, you'll frighten them and I want to hear them talk. Take your sun-bonnets off and I'll give you some of the milk to drink.

BETHIA. Oh, we never drink that kind. Mother skims it on purpose for you.

SOPHIA. Yes, on purpose for you.

BERNICE. I read in ancient history once, that children and fools are noted for their veracity.

LAURA. What makes your mother take so much trouble for us ?

BETHIA. She said city folks wasn't used to good milk and it would make 'em sick.

SOPHIA. Awful sick !

CLARICE. Thoughtful soul !

BERNICE. What's your name, bright eyes ?

BETHIA. Bethia Maria Hardstratch.

LAURA. And yours, curly-locks.

SOPHIA. No, it hain't Curly-locks. It's jest Sophia Zeniah Hardscratch.

EDITH. Simply that and nothing more.

BETHIA. Mother's awful glad you're campin' out, 'cause Miss Dexter don' keep hens and cows, an' mother says she'll make a lot of money out of you.

SOPHIA. Lots of money.

BETHIA. You've got fixed up real nice out here, hain't you ? It's ever so much nicer than stayin' in doors. I jest hate goin' to school !

SOPHIA. Hate it !

LAURA. That's naughty. (*Recites in high-pitched monotones.*) " You should love your teachers fond and true, and help them all you can, Some little act each day should do—should do—— Some one help me, can't you ?

BETHIA. Humph ! I don't believe *you'd* like to go to school, if all the boys called you twinsey.

SOPHIA. Yes, jest hollered " twinsey."

BETHIA. And said your pa was hen-pecked.

SOPHIA. Hen-pecked ! Jimmy True said that, and I jest told him 'twan't no such thing, for Bethia an me got all the eggs and pa didn't go near the hens.

EDITH.   Wise man !   Keep away from the hens.

BETHIA.   Pa's awful good, an' said ·he was sorry for you, 'cause ma was jest roastin' you.

SOPHIA.   Yes, he did say it ; roastin' you !

BERNICE.   Oh, where's my camera ?   I must get a snap-shot at the twins !

LAURA.   Even the innocence of childhood escapeth not !

[*Exit* BERNICE R.

SOPHIA.   What's she gone to fetch ?

EDITH.   A camera.   Wait, she's going to take your picture.

Re-enter BERNICE *with camera.*

SOPHIA.   Won't it go off ?

BERNICE.   Not very far.   Now you must hold still, or you'll spoil the picture.   You mustn't move a bit.

BETHIA.   If I should. wiggle my toe in my shoe, would it spoil the picture ?

BERNICE.   Sure !   Now, then, smile a little. (*They grin.*)   All right !   You come down in a few day and I'll show it to you.

BETHIA.   Is that all there is to it ?

SOPHIA.   All there is ?

BERNICE.   Yes.

BETHIA.   Humph ! it didn't hurt a bit.

LAURA.   That's because you didn't move.

BETHIA.   I didn't do nothin'.

SOPHIA.   I bit my tongue, will that show ?

BERNICE.   No, I won't let it.

BETHIA.   Come on, Sophia, we must go now, or mother'll say we stayed long enough to tell everything we know, an' I hain't told half, have you ?

SOPHIA.   No, not half!   Hain't told how eggs is fell to eighteen cents a dozen, nor how mother dropped the butter out of the pail an' scraped it, nor nothin'.

LAURA.   That's right, don't tell !   (*Girls laugh.*)   Here's a bag of candy for you.   (*Gives candy to* BETHIA.)   Come again.

ALL.   Good-bye.

BETHIA *and* SOPHIA.   Good-bye.

LAURA.   You don't have to go on the lake for an echo.

AUNT DEBBY *enters* R. *with work-basket
and stockings to darn.*

BERNICE.   Here, Aunt Debby, take this seat.   I'm glad

you're going to sit down. (AUNT DEBBY *sits up* C.) For I'm afraid this camping trip is making you a lot of work.

[*Girls all sit around her.*

CLARICE. How good it was of you to let us come!

AUNT DEBBY. Why, my dear girls, I've enjoyed every moment of it.

EDITH. It has been a happy summer.

LAURA. There hasn't been one thing to mar our pleasure, not one!

EDITH (*aside*). None of them know how Clare's heart aches, and how she tries to hide it.

BERNICE. It's worth a good deal to know your future, and old Clem has told us just what to expect. Laura, every time I look at at you and think you're going to have three husbands, I can forgive anything you may do. Just think! one commits suicide, another gets a divorce and the third runs away!

LAURA. Well, you aren't going to have any, miss!

BERNICE. For which I am duly thankful. Edith's going to marry the first man who asks her, and Clarice, poor girl, has got to go through fire and water, before she " lives in grease and dies in peace, and is buried in a pot of cream."

Enter ELINOR, R. *with pan of pop-corn.*

ELINOR (*calling*). Hot popped corn! popped corn!

CLARICE. You're an angel, Elinor! Here, set the pan in front of us, and we'll eat, while Aunt Debby darns. (ELINOR *sets pan in* C.; *all sit around it.*) Doesn't it seem strange to have such a lot of harum-scarum girls, calling you. " Aunt Debby "?

AUNT DEBBY. It pleases me more than I can tell you, child.

ELINOR. Aunt Debby's heart is fairly bubbling over with love; and it would be a pity to have any of it go to waste; so it's lucky you are where you can catch it as it falls.

LAURA. A pretty metaphor, Elinor, but if you go on like that, you'll have a headache.

BERNICE. You must remember, my dear, that some people can stand a mental strain, that would kill others. Now, don't try to answer me! Your mouth is too full of corn.

EDITH (*looking off* R.). Oh, I say, girls, there is the funniest looking woman I ever saw coming this way!

AUNT DEBBY. Who can it be, I wonder. [*Girls rise.*

ELINOR (*looking*). No one I've ever seen before.

LAURA. She looks as if her clothes had been thrown at her and caught on here and there, just as it happened.

CLARICE. Look at her baggage! She has come to stay, wherever she is going.

ELINOR. Stand back, girls, here she comes !

[*Girls fall back.*

Enter MEHITIBLE DOOLITTLE, R. *She carries an old-fashioned carpet-bag, hand-satchel, band-box and umbrella.*

MEHITIBLE. Wall, I swan ! if I hain't run right into a camp.

AUNT DEBBY (*rising*). Don't be startled, my good woman, we are quite harmless. Have you lost your way ?

MEHITIBLE. You've hit it now. I got off the cars an' thought I'd cut across lots to Deacon Hardscratch's an' I run right into this ere place.

ELINOR. Sit down and rest yourself.

AUNT DEBBY. Yes, you look tired. Bring her a glass of lemonade, Elinor. [*Exit* ELINOR R.

MEHITIBLE (*sits* R.). I run ! I never was so beat out in my life. Do you know the Hardscratches, marm ?

AUNT DEBBY. Oh, yes, they are near neighbors of ours, and you are only a short distance from their house. The twins were here only a little while ago.

MEHITIBLE. Want to know if the twins was here ! Bright as buttons, ain't they ? I'm Mrs. Hardscratch's sister, Mehitible Doolittle.

AUNT DEBBY Oh, yes, I've heard her speak of you often.

MEHITIBLE. I writ her I was comin' over from Peakville, a week ago ; but I had a lot of salve to box, an' couldn't get away a minit sooner. Be these girls all yours ?

AUNT DEBBY. No, they are spending the summer with me, and we came here to camp for a little outing.

Enter ELINOR, R., *with lemonade, which* MEHITIBLE *drinks eagerly.*

MEHITIBLE. Thank you ; that touches the right spot.

CLARICE (*offering fan*). Perhaps you'd like a fan, Miss Doo-
..ttle.

MEHITIBLE. Wall, I don't care if I do. I was pretty nigh unsettled before I took the cars, for I'd been packin yarbs all the mornin' an' the sun was scorchin.' So you're campin' out ? I never could see any fun in it. Jest give me a good feather-bed when night comes.

AUNT DEBBY. We have found it very pleasant. We came to these woods because we could get some of the provisions from your sister's farm.

MEHITIBLE. Want to know if Samanthy's lettin' you have supplies ! That'll be a reg'lar picnic for her.

EDITH (*to* CLARICE). Evidently she knows Samanthy's little weakness.

MEHITIBLE. Yes, she's got a master-head for business, Samanthy has, an' it's got to be mighty poor pickin' when she don't make money.

AUNT DEBBY. Yes, Mrs. Hardscratch is a very thrifty woman.

MEHITIBLE. The deacon, poor critter, I kinder pity him!

BERNICE (*to* LAURA). So do I!

MEHITIBLE. I hain't seen him for two years. His hair was thinnin' out awful fast, an' he had a terrible meachin' look, that spoke for itself.

EDITH (*to* CLARICE). That was evidently while she was "a trainin' him."

MEHITIBLE. Samanthy was quite set up when she ketched the deacon, for none of us had any idea she'd ever marry; but somehow or nuther the Doolittles all got married, sooner or later.

AUNT DEBBY. And yet you are single.

MEHITIBLE. Wall, I shan't be long.

BERNICE (*to* LAURA). "Lives there a man with heart so dead?"

AUNT DEBBY. Well, I hope your choice will be a wise one, Miss Doolittle. Your sister told me you were quite a nurse; that you manufactured bitters, ointments, tonics, and the like.

MEHITIBLE. La, yes, I make 'em by the gallon. Ain't any of you troubled with rheumatiz, be you? I've got a liniment that will cure it quicker'n you can say "Jack Robinson."

AUNT DEBBY. Mrs. Hardscratch makes medicine, too. She sent one of the girls a bottle of it.

CLARICE. The cat knocked the bottle over, lapped some of it, and died in spasms.

MEHITIBLE. Too bad it was wasted on the cat!

EDITH. Yes, wasn't it a shame?

MEHITIBLE. You speak as if you had catarrh. Now let me tell you something about my catarrh snuff. Elder Snitkins, down to the Centre, had catarrh so't he'd sneeze an' blow, an' sneeze, until he'd get every one in the meetin'-house a-blowin' too; an' he couldn't beat religion into them critters to save his life. Hadn't no voice at all, scarcely. Of course, when he found his voice goin', he'd beat the pulpit with his fist all the harder; then the dust would fly an' set him to sneezin', like a cat that had stuck her nose into cayenne pepper—only the elder'd sneeze so loud he'd make the shandyleers tremble. Wall, one day I persuaded him to try a box of my snuff, an' he hadn't taken six boxes before his head was clear as a bell, an' he could holler like a loon.

BERNICE. Poor man! how grateful he must have been!

MEHITIBLE. Yes, he seemed to be, an' said seein' as how I'd done so much for *him*, if I was willin' to undertake the job of doctorin' his seven children, all of 'em bein' pindlin', he'd marry me.

LAURA.   So the elder proposed !

MEHITIBLE.   Yes ; he said I could keep right on makin' bitters, salves, an' such, an' as fast as the children took sick, I could try it on 'em, an' if it cured 'em I should have a free conscience to sell it to other people.

ELINOR.   And what if it killed them ?

MEHITIBLE.   Then they'd be buried 'longside of their mother, poor things !   The elder has a beautiful corner lot.   [Sighs.

LAURA.   And when is the wedding to be, Miss Doolittle ?

MEHITIBLE.   In about four weeks.   I came down to Samanthy's to make the cake.   She'll be dretful surprised, for she didn't mistrust a thing about it.   (Rising.)   Wall, I might as well be pokin' along.   Hope I shan't get lost again.

AUNT DEBBY.   Wait a minute, Miss Doolittle, we will see if we can't find Ashrael.   She will show you the way.   Elinor, just blow that horn, and if she's anywhere about, she'll hear you.   I don't see where she can be !   [ELINOR blows horn.

LAURA.   I met her and Fantine, just as Bernice and I were coming in ; they can't be far.

BERNICE.   I am afraid I shall have to get rid of Fantine when I leave here.   She is a perfectly useless appendage and never about when I want her.

Enter ASHRAEL *and* FANTINE, *out of breath*, R.

AUNT DEBBY.   Where in the world did you hide yourself, Ashrael ?   I have wanted you several times.

ASHRAEL.   I was down by the spring, readin' to Fantine.   I tried to have her run up to camp, to see if you wanted anything, but she was so scairt at Black Donald's ghost, she wouldn't stir an inch.

BERNICE.   Who's ghost ?

ASHRAEL.   Oh, jest in the book miss !

FANTINE.   Oh, it was terreeble !   A ghost who was all bones !

LAURA.   Did you expect him to look fat and healthy ?

BERNICE.   Don't fill her foolish head with any more such tales, Ashrael.

ASHRAEL.   All right, miss, I didn't know she was so weak in the brain.

AUNT DEBBY.   Ashrael, this is Mrs. Hardscratch's sister. Show her where she lives.   She has lost her way.   Go as far as Lover's Lane ; she can see the house there.

ASHRAEL.   Yes'm.   Right this way.   [Going L.

MEHITIBLE.   I'm turrible obleeged to you for your perliteness.

AUNT DEBBY.   Don't mention it.   Come down and see us again.

MEHITIBLE. I'll try to, an' if any of you come this way another year, jest drive over to Peakville Centre, an' call on Mrs. Elder Snifkins.

LAURA. Thank you, Miss Doolittle ; we'll surely come.

EDITH. Indeed we will !

ELINOR. I hope you'll cure the elder's children ?

CLARICE. Yes, and be happy with the elder.

ALL. Good-bye !

MEHITIBLE. Good-bye ! [*Exit with* ASHRAEL.

BERNICE. That's a character study for you, girls.

LAURA. The queerest we've seen yet.

BERNICE. Fantine, you may mend my serge skirt. I am going boating after tea and shall need it.

FANTINE. Vera well, mademoiselle. (*Aside.*) I shall not prick my fingers vera long for you. [*Exit* R.

EDITH. Well, I'm off to beautify myself for my drive with Dick.

CLARICE. Don't make yourself too lovely.

EDITH. No danger. I wish you were going too, Clare.

CLARICE. There, there, don't fib.

EDITH. I'm not fibbing ! You won't get blue, will you ?

CLARICE. Don't worry, dear ; haven't you seen how I've been " cutting up," as Ashrael says.

EDITH (*arm about her*). I know you are trying to be a brave little girl, and——

LAURA. No secrets, Edith ! Remember, you are going to tell us all Dick says when you get back.

EDITH. Of course, every word.

LAURA. No cheating.

EDITH. " Honest and true ; cross myself." [*Exit* R.

BERNICE. She grows prettier every day.

AUNT DEBBY. She's a dear, thoughtful child. There, Elinor, the stockings are mended. Now, if you'll hand me that pan of apples (*pointing off stage* R.) I'll pare a few for an apple-float while I sit here.

[*Exit* ELINOR, R., *returning with apples.*

LAURA. You are never idle a moment, Aunt Debby.

BERNICE. How can she be idle ? Look at the hungry girls she has to feed.

ELINOR. I can just tell you if you didn't have good appetites, Aunt Debby would feel personally injured.

AUNT DEBBY. Nothing pleases me more than——

[*Scream heard outside,* OLD CLEM *shouting,* " *Run, ye imps of Satan ! If I had my hands on ye, I'd throttle ye like vermin, as ye are!*" *She staggers on* L. *with bundle of baskets, her arm bleeding.*

GIRLS. It's the old gipsy !

AUNT DEBBY (*rising*).   And she's hurt!
ELINOR.   Poor old Clem!   Your arm is bleeding.   (*Leads her to seat,* R.)   Who hurt you?
CLEM.   Those boys, the black-hearted little torments, stretched a string across my path, then hid and watched me fall.
BERNICE.   What a shame!
GIRLS.   How cruel!
ELINOR.   I will bathe your arm, Clem.   It must hurt you badly.
[*Exit* R.*, returning with basin of water, sponge and bandage, and dresses arm.*

AUNT DEBBY.   Those boys should be punished for doing a thing like that.   [*Exit* R.
CLARICE.   That's not sport!
LAURA.   It's sheer cruelty.
BERNICE.   Let me take your baskets.   [*Places them up* L.
CLEM.   Oh, I'd like to wind my fingers round their throats, I'd——
ELINOR (*bandaging arm*).   There, there, don't get so angry, Clem!
CLEM.   Angry?   It isn't the arm that hurts, that's nothing. It's the feeling here, (*hand on heart*) they give me, those rich men's sons!   I'd like to see 'em beg from door to door, starving, freezing!
ELINOR.   Oh, Clem, don't!
CLEM.   I'd crush 'em, like worms under my heel, an' I'd rack their bones with pain, 'till they'd cry for mercy.   Curse 'em! When did they ever try to do a kindness for me?   They laugh and jeer at me, and throw rocks at me!   Nobody cares for old Clem, but she can make 'em rue this day, if she *is* old!   Snakes shall bite 'em and wasps sting 'em!
ELINOR.   I care for you, Clem, and I'd do anything for you. We'll buy all your baskets and——
CLEM (*bursting into tears*).   Don't! don't!
AUNT DEBBY (*entering* R. *with glass of wine*).   Here, my poor woman, drink some wine, you are trembling with exhaustion.
ELINOR (*giving her glass*).   Yes, do drink it!   I am sure it will make you better.   (*Going* L.)   Now, girls, select your baskets.   Aren't they pretty?
BERNICE.   Let us see how many there are.   Aunt Debby must have this for her mending.
CLEM (*talking to herself*).   She dressed that bony old arm, with her white fingers.   She wasn't afraid of the old gipsy's blood, and she said that she cared for me.
CLARICE.   Clem's talking to herself.
ELINOR.   Yes, she's getting quiet.   Don't notice her.
CLEM.   Nobody's said that for years.

BERNICE (*smelling baskets*). How fragrant this sweet grass
is !

ELINOR. You must accept this for your handkerchiefs.

CLEM (*becoming delirious*). Is that you calling, Harry?
I hurried from camp, as fast as I could. What makes you look
so grave, dear? Sit at my feet with your head in my lap and
let me stroke your curls. Light, sunny curls, I love them so !

BERNICE. She's mumbling to herself yet.

ELINOR. She's very weak to-day.

[*Girls talk during* CLEM'S *soliliquy.*

CLEM (*moaning*). Oh, Harry ! your father said that ? No,
no lad, I'll never ruin your life. Don't ask me ! They can take
you from the poor gipsy girl, but I—I——

[*Head sinks on breast.*

AUNT DEBBY (*going to her and trying to rouse her*). Clem !
Clem ! come into the tent and lie down. You're ill, I fear.

CLEM. No, I—I'm all right.

ELINOR (*assisting her to rise*). Please go in and rest, just to
please me, won't you ?

CLEM. What does it matter to you ?

ELINOR, Very much. It hurts me to see you like this,
Clem.

CLEM. And the sight of your face, the sound of your voice,
hurts me worse than the rocks they throw at me. (*Going.*)
Yes, I'll go to please you, I'll go. [*Exit* R., ELINOR *leading her.*

CLARICE. What an influence Elinor has over that old
woman !

AUNT DEBBY. She has known her for years and could always
make her do anything. When she was a little girl, Clem would
come up to Breezy Point and sit watching her at play, for
hours. And once, when Elinor was sick, she wouldn't leave
the house and acted like an insane woman.

BERNICE, Then Elinor has lived with you since she was a
child ?

AUNT DEBBY. Yes.

LAURA. Are both her parents dead ?

AUNT DEBBY. I'm the nearest relative she has. [*Exit* R.

LAURA. I'll wager there's some mystery about Elinor.

CLARICE. Life is full of them.

BERNICE. There have been more facts than fancies in my
life, at any rate.

LAURA. Poor girl ! You have had some sad experiences,
haven't you ?

BERNICE (*gravely*). A few, dear.

LAURA. I often think what a shock it must have been to you
to find yourself practically alone in a strange city with a sick
father. How long did he live after you landed ?

BERNICE. Three months, three *precious* months, for he gave·me counsel in those few weeks to direct me all my life.

CLARICE. And haven't you any relatives in this country, Bernice, not one?

BERNICE. Not any, dear, nor in the wide world, except an uncle in England, whom I have never seen. But then, you know, my guardian was papa's friend and he is very kind to me.

LAURA. ˙And then you have loads of money—and there's me! I'm going to stick to you like grim death, for I haven't any sister and my mother has so many clubs and societies to attend that I always feel as if I were trespassing on her time when I am at home. I'm sure she'll find it pretty hard to be quarantined while Jack has scarlet fever.

BERNICE (*embracing her*). A girl couldn't be very lonely who had you. Only you'll be falling in love one of these days, and leaving me.

LAURA. Never! we'll be girl bachelors and keep an ideal hall. But come on, let's interview the speckled beauties in Bow Brook.

BERNICE. There is no bait.

LAURA. I'll dig some. I'm not a bit afraid of those nasty, wriggling worms now, and I take positive delight in stringing them on a hook. (*Picks up tomato-can.*) Here's the bait-box. Just come and watch me. Aren't you coming, Clarice?

CLARICE. No. I've letters to write, and then, I always scare the fish.

BERNICE. Well, we'll catch a trout for your supper, then.

LAURA. Yes, I'll bring you a half-pounder.

[*Exeunt* LAURA *and* BERNICE L.

CLARICE. They're as good as gold, those girls! Oh, there's the sound of carriage wheels! (*Looks off* R.) Yes, Dick has come for Edith. How pretty she looks in that blue gown and hat with pink roses! Dick has won her heart, there's no doubt about that. I hope he can be trusted with it! (*Sits* R.) I should be sorry to see her make such an idiot of herself as I have done! Dick was Charlie Grierson's sworn chum. I wonder if he knows his whereabouts. Nonsense! here I am again, wasting my thoughts on a man I ought to hate! But it's no use. I never eat an apple but I find myself saving the seeds and saying; "One, I love," and all that folderol. This very morning, I picked a daisy, and, before I knew it, I was counting the petals. (*Rises.*) Clarice Fenleigh, you're a little fool, and you've got to stop such actions! Now I'll go and write a letter to my mother, and tell her how happy I am; and I'll make her believe it if I don't.   [*Exit* R.

Enter FANTINE, L., *with valise, hat, and jacket, looking
cautiously around.*

FANTINE. They haf all gone, and I shall work no more.
You can leenish to sew your skirt yourself, Mademoiselle Verenon! I shall nevare thread some needles for you some more.
Let me see what zey is all about. (*Looks off* R.) Ze old lady
and her niece are some berries peeking ofer, and zey haf a half
pan yet to peek. I know zey old geepsy is ' asleep, for I did
hear her snore with her nose. My meestress and her friend haf
gone, with a shovel, to deeg some worms out of the ground, and
Mees Fenleigh is writing. I must hurry myself, for I shall haf
only the time to lose Ashreel and get to the veelage. (*Takes
letter from pocket and pins it on tree up* R.) Mees Ashreel
Grant, zere is a lettare for you, and you will nevare say some
more zat I haf no brains inside my head. (*Puts on hat.*) Let
me see if haf forgot sometings. (*Looks in valise.*) How vera
bright in me to get my wages for ze month, last night! I tells
mademoiselle I wants to buy me some shoes. Yes, everyting I
shall need me is here. Zey will be surprised vera mooch to
find me when I am gone. Ah, zey think I am vera—what zey
call ze color of ze leaf? Ah, oui, green! but I knows sometings, or two. Now I am ready to say good-bye, but I shall
wheesper it, so no ones shall hear me.

    [*Throws kiss mockingly to* R., *waves handkerchief and
exit* L., *cautiously.*

Enter ELINOR, R. *with large basket, places it up* L.

ELINOR. There! Clem mustn't forget her basket when she
goes back to camp. Poor old woman! she was worn out. I
fear she is failing. What a life she leads! But there is one good
thing about it, there is not one of the tribe but fear her, and so
she is treated well. They think she has the power of casting an
evil spell over any one, and that the fairies, good and bad, obey
her will. (*Looks off* L.) Here comes Ashrael; I was just
thinking it was time she returned.

Enter ASHRAEL, L., *reading aloud.*

ASHRAEL. "' Advance another step and you lie dead at my
feet!' said Gwendoline, and as she looked into those dark,
burning eyes, the white jewelled hand that held the revolver,
dropped lifelessly at her side." Pshaw! she hadn't the spunk of
a mouse. These folks that are always threatenin' to shoot
never do it. It used to scare me some when Billy——(*Discovers* ELINOR.) Ah, are you there, Miss Elinor? I didn't see
you.

ELINOR. No, you were too busy reading. What makes you
read such stuff as that, Ashrael?

ASHRAEL. Oh, I likes it. It makes me feel all shivery !

ELINOR. Is that a pleasant feeling ? But how about your sweetheart, Billy Griffin ? I haven't heard you talk much about him lately.

ASHRAEL. I hain't seen him alone, 'cause that French greenie is at my heels most of the time, but he's jest the same, I reckon. He's quiet, but I know he's desprit.

ELINOR. Still going to shoot himself ?

ASHRAEL. Oh, yes, I s'pose so.

ELINOR. What a dreadful thing it would be if he should !

ASHRAEL. Yes, of course, it would be ruther bad, but 'twould advertise me well. Jest think how it would look in the papers ! A picture of Billy, with a revolver in his hand, on one side, an' me on the other with " Ashrael Grant, the girl he died for," in big letters over my head.

Enter LAURA *and* BERNICE, R.

LAURA. What a shame you had to catch your skirt on that hateful old nail, just as we were ready to start ! Halloo, Elinor ! Bernice is up for repairs.

ELINOR. Here is Aunt Debby's basket ; I'll fix it for you in a minute.   [*Girls up* R. ELINOR *kneels and sews braid on* BERNICE'S *skirt.*

ASHRAEL (*going up* R.). Well, I guess I'll go in an' see if I can help Miss Dexter. (*Discovers letter on tree.*) For the land sakes ! what's that letter up there for ? (*Taking it down.*) " Miss Ashreel Grant." Why, what in the world does that imp want to write to me for ? Goodness knows I see enough of her without writin' ! but she don't know much an' I hadn't orter expect she'd act as if she had common sense. She's so simple you can read her as easy as if she was made of glass. (*Opens letter and reads.*) " My poor Ashreel " :—Poor ! well, I like that, " You called me a greenhorn, but I haf made one big fool of you." What in the world is she trying to get at ? " I haf stolen your little Billie, and we shall be m-married to-night."

[*She stands perfectly rigid, closes eyes, hands clenched, and gives a succession of shrill, sharp screams.* AUNT DEBBY *and* CLARICE *rush in, girls surround her.*

ALL. What is it, Ashrael ?   [*She continues to scream.*

AUNT DEBBY (*shaking her*). Speak, Ashraél ! Tell me what is the matter!

ASHRAEL. They've run away ! Gone to be married !

ELINOR. Who ? Who has run away ?

ASHRAEL. That French fiend has stolen my beau ! Pursue 'em ! handcuff 'em ! gag 'em !

ALL. Fantine !

ASHRAEL. Yes, that little wrigglin' snake has swiped Billy Griffin right from under my nose ! And him a-goin' to shoot himself 'cause I wouldn't have him, the miserable little red-headed varmint !

BERNICE. Fantine run away ?

ASHRAEL. Yes, I tell you, gone, hide an' hair of 'em !

[BERNICE *and* LAURA *run off* R., ASHRAEL *walking stage and wringing hands.*

AUNT DEBBY. Sit down, Ashrael, and be quiet ; calm yourself.

ASHRAEL. I can't calm myself ! I won't !

ELINOR. What makes you feel so, Ashrael ? You didn't want him.

ASHRAEL. Well, I didn't intend anyone else should have him ! And there that critter was a-sneakin out to meet him nights, an' a-tellin me she went to look at the moon !

CLARICE. Poor Ashrael !

ASHRAEL. Don't call me that, them's her words ! " Poor Ashreel ! "

Re-enter BERNICE *and* LAURA R. BERNICE, AUNT DEBBY *and* ELINOR *talk apart up* R.

CLARICE. No man is worth grieving for like that, Ashrael.

ASHRAEL. It hain't so much the man, but it's the shame of havin' the wool pulled over your eyes like that ; 'specially by a little measly furriner ! Oh, I'd jest like to get my hands on to 'em ! I'd scratch her eyes out and make him bald-headed in less'n five minutes ! I'd——

BERNICE (*going to her*). Ashrael, listen to me, please. I am so sorry for you, indeed, I am !

ASHRAEL. Well, you needn't be ! He's the stingiest thing alive ! Gave me a ring once and it turned my finger black as ink !

BERNICE. I was completely deceived in Fantine.

ASHRAEL. I wasn't ! I knew she was a villian of the deepest dye. Oh, I'd jest like to use her for a dish-rag ! The little idjit, to leave a place like she had for a low-born butcher ! But I fooled her ! She thought he was a doctor. A doctor ! he don't know enough to pick the feathers off a hen !

BERNICE. Ashrael, how would you like to take Fantine's place ?

ASHRAEL. What, run away with him ?

BERNICE. No, stay with me.

ASHRAEL. Huh ?

BERNICE. How would you like to take Fantine's place and go to Paris with me ?

3

ASHRAEL. To Paris? Me, go to Paris? Somebody set a chair for me, quick! I know I shall faint—go to Paris!

BERNICE. Aunt Debby is willing.

AUNT DEBBY. It's a great chance for you, Ashrael.

ELINOR. The chance of your life.

ASHRAEL. Hooray! to Paris! She's welcome to all the Billy Griffins from here to Canada line! You mean it, miss? no foolin'?

BERNICE. I am very much in earnest, Ashrael.

ASHRAEL. Well, there's my hand! I'll stick to you through thick an' thin! And when we comes back from our travels, we'll show 'em the stuff American citizens are made of!

[ASHRAEL *and* BERNICE C. AUNT DEBBY *seated* R., ELINOR *standing by her*, LAURA L. *with arm about* CLARICE.

CURTAIN.

————

ACT III.

SCENE.—*Same as Act I. Four weeks later. Bell on table* R., *hat on couch* L. CLARICE *discovered* R. *of table reading.*

Enter ELINOR L.

ELINOR. There! I don't believe even Aunt Debby could beat that frosting. Oh! you are here, Clarice. I thought you had gone to the post-office.

CLARICE. No, Edith went and the girls wouldn't let me do one thing in the kitchen. Laura chased me out with the broom and Bernice threw a pan of pea-pods after me.

ELINOR (*laughing*). You ought to see them! Bernice has made some cream-cakes and Laura has started on a new receipt. The way she beats eggs would develop a regular base-ball muscle. (*Sits* L., *at small table.*) I feel as though I were in a dream every time I look at them, with their sleeves rolled up, working in the kitchen, upstairs, all over the house. Wasn't it aggravating that the cook's cousin's boy should break his leg the very next day after Aunt Debby went away?

CLARICE. I think it has been glorious fun keeping house; only there isn't work enough to go 'round, with so many to help.

LAURA (*at door* L., *sleeves rolled up, flour on nose*). Where is the vanilla, Elinor?

ELINOR. Beside the package of corn-starch on the second shelf. I'm coming right out and——

LAURA. No, you shan't ! I'm nervous when I try a new receipt. I've just sent Bernice upstairs. [*Exit.*

CLARICE. You see, Elinor, you are a sort of side issue in your own house.

ELINOR. You are all so good to me ! When I think your vacation is over and you are only staying here to keep me company, while Aunt Debby is gone, and that you are risking Madame Finikin's displeasure, it makes me feel guilty. I am afraid your vacation will be anything but a rest.

CLARICE. We promised Aunt Debby, of our own accord, not to leave until she returned. Bernice and Laura are not going back to school and it will make but little difference if Edith and I miss a few weeks. She gets her tuition just the same, and that is what the madame is looking after. But, I say, Elinor, hasn't it been rather lively about here for a fortnight ? My head has been in a perfect whirl ever since we got back from camp, two weeks ago. Fantine started the ball rolling when she eloped with Ashrael's beau.

ELINOR. That was a blessing in disguise ; but when old Clem came up here one day, and was taken sick and died, that cast a shadow over us all.

CLARICE. And the next day Aunt Debby was called away.

ELINOR. She wouldn't even tell me where she was going. I cannot think why she acted like that, so quiet and strange ; she was never that way with me before. [*Wiping eyes.*

CLARICE (*going to her*). There, Elinor, don't grieve over it ! You are the apple of Aunt Debby's eye, and you may be sure there was some good reason for her silence. May be it was some business that she thought might worry you.

ELINOR. I am almost sure of that.

CLARICE. Haven't you any idea where she has gone ?

ELINOR. Yes, Aunt Debby's brother died, out in Kansas, last winter, and his affairs were badly involved. I feel almost sure that she was sent for to go there ; and if there was anything wrong she would not tell me until she was obliged to do so. But if she knew that the hired help had deserted us, and that you girls had been working, she would be ill with anxiety.

CLARICE. Why do you give yourself so much uneasiness about the work ? (*Sits* L. *of table.*) It has been absolute fun ! and although I was sorry for Jane when she was " took with a felon," yet if she *had* to be " took," I was glad it was at that time.

Enter BERNICE L.

BERNICE. Laura puts on all the airs of a French cook. She has even chased the cat out of the kitchen, for fear she would jar the stove and make the cake fall.

ELINOR. And here I am resting, while she is at work!

BERNICE. Work? Why it's the opportunity of her life to show us how much she learned at cooking-school last winter. Well, there is a certain kind of excitement when she tries a new dish; to see if it kills any of us. [*Sits* R. *of table.*

ELINOR (*laughing*). The only trouble is that she makes everything so good it doesn't last, and it keeps her cooking all the time.

CLARICE. She made a fatal mistake yesterday morning. The twins called, and Laura had just made a dozen tartlets; they eyed them hungrily, so our dear little cook says: "Help yourselves, my dears;" and they did, for not a tartlet remained to tell the tale!

ELINOR (*laughing*). No doubt they were sick all night, and Mrs. Hardscratch dosed them with thoroughwort tea. But where is Ashrael! I haven't seen her this morning.

BERNICE. I sent her to the village for some things. I have been making a note of everything I heard any one express a wish for, and I started her off bright and early. It is time she returned. [*Rises, looks off* C.

CLARICE (*laughing*). Isn't she proud of her new position?

BERNICE. It is a great satisfaction to me that I was able to recompense her somewhat for the loss of her sweetheart.

ELINOR. Poor Ashrael! She has always been "aspirin'," and the thought of going to Paris nearly intoxicates her. You were born there, were you not, Bernice?

BERNICE. Yes, it was my home until I was twelve years old; then mamma died and papa never wanted to see the place again. (*Sits on hassock by* ELINOR.) For several years we travelled incessantly, always trying to find some nook where he would be content. Ah, how he loved my pretty golden-haired mother! I have seen him sit for hours with her picture in his hand, gazing at it so tenderly, and whispering such loving words that, child as I was, I would creep into a corner and cry for him, as much as for myself.

ELINOR. Poor little girl!

BERNICE. Then he would call me to him, take my face in his hands, and kiss my forehead and my eyes, because they were like my mother's, he would say. I had an old nurse, but she was garrulous and her constant chatter fretted him, so I was alone with him most of the time.

CLARICE. How did you learn so much, Bernice, flitting, as you were, from place to place? I remember when you came to Madame Finikin's, you were in advance of nearly all the girls.

BERNICE. My father taught me faithfully. He was the closest student I ever knew, and when I was very small he nearly always spoke to me in German or Italian, and old Mathilde was French, so I was versed in those languages very young.

ELINOR. Was he an invalid, Bernice?

BERNICE. Not until my mother died; then life seemed but a weary waiting until he should join her. His only regret was in leaving me; but after we came to New York, and he found Mr. Livingstone, a friend of his boyhood, who consented to become my guardian, and in whom my father had implicit confidence, a great burden was lifted from him and he gave up his life, day by day, so happily.

ELINOR. It must have been so sad for you, Bernice, to know he was slipping from you!

BERNICE. Sometimes, at twilight, I would sit by his bedside, with my head on his pillow, and he would say: "May be before another month I shall see your mother, dear." I shall never forget the night he died. He was delirious, and in fancy he was wooing my mother. He seemed to be walking with her in some lovely lane, where the trees were full of blossoms and the birds sang in their branches. I remember seeing him reach up to pick their blossoms, and then he would try to fashion them into a wreath for her hair. He said: "Hear that linnet sing! He is pleading my cause, Janette."

ELINOR (stroking her hair). Poor Bernice! it was terrible for you!

BERNICE. Just before he died he asked her to become his wife. I shall never forget the expression on his face, as he seemed to catch her answer and, raising his arms, he folded something to his breast that our eyes could not see, and murmuring, "Sweetheart, naught shall divide us," he gently breathed his last.

ELINOR. I am afraid this recital has pained you, Bernice.

BERNICE (rises). No. It is always a pleasure to speak of my father. He was so happy to go, I would not have detained him if I could. I have much to be grateful for, much to make me happy.

Enter LAURA L.

LAURA. It's done, and it's a dream!

CLARICE. What? [Rises.

LAURA. The cake.

CLARICE. I'm afraid we will find it a reality that will be a heavy burden.

BERNICE. Maybe we will have the dream after we eat it.

LAURA. You just say two more words, either of you, and you shan't have a morsel! You shall just look on and watch the rest of us eat it. [Knock at door, L.

ELINOR (rises). Come in.

Enter the HARDSCRATCH TWINS, L.

BETHIA.   Ma sent us over to see if we could help you any.
SOPHIA.   Do let us help you !
ELINOR.   My dear little girls, we are fairly over run with help.
BERNICE (*to* ELINOR).   See how disappointed they look ! We must find something for them to do.
ELINOR.   Take your sun-bonnets off, and I will see what I can do for you.   [*Exit* L.; *the* TWINS *sit on couch.*
CLARICE.   Why aren't you at school, girls ?
BETHIA.   The teacher's feller has got a fever, and she's gone for a week.   She's got Lorinda Holmes to take her place, and mother says she don't know beans, so we needn't go to school til teacher gets back.
BERNICE (*laughing*).   Oh, I see.
BETHIA.   Mother fairly hates the Holmeses !   When the fair was down to Gallville, last year, mother sent a quilt with nine hundred and ninety-nine pieces in it an' some pickled pears. Lorinda Holmes sent a quilt with a thousand pieces an' she took the prize.
SOPHIA.   An' her pickled pears had cloves stuck in 'em, an' mother's didn't, so she took the prize on them too, an'- mother hain't spoke to her sence.   [*Girls laugh.*

Re-enter ELINOR L. *with an earthen dish, knife and dish of raisins.*

ELINOR.   Here, girls, I've found something for you to do. (*Arranges chairs for them,* C.) Sit here and stone these raisins. (*Exit* BERNICE C. TWINS *sit* C.)   Let me show you how to do it.   Pull them apart, so, and take the seeds out with this little knife, like that.
BETHIA.   Oh, that's easy !
SOPHIA.   Awful easy !

Re-enter BERNICE C., *with dress-skirt on arm.*

BERNICE.   And when you have finished, run into the kitchen and wash your hands carefully, then you may rip the binding off this skirt. (*Puts it on chair* R.)   You will find two pairs of scissors in the work-basket, on the table.
BETHIA.   We know how to do that, don't we, Sophia ?
SOPHIA.   Yes, that ain't nothin' ; we rip all of mother's clothes to make over for us.
ELINOR.   Well, I'm going to tie up that rose-vine, over the porch.
CLARICE.   I'll go with you.
          [*Exeunt* CLARICE *and* ELINOR. C.

LAURA. Come on, Bernice, let's lie in the hammock, and see if it is artistically done. (*Picking hat up from couch.*) No, I shan't need my hat.   [*Throws it again on couch.*

BERNICE. Who ever heard of a hat in a hammock!

LAURA. Well, I can imagine occasions when they might be in the way.   [*Exeunt* LAURA *and* BERNICE C. *laughing.*

BETHIA. Give me half of 'em in my apron, an' you take the other half, then we can each of us have a dish to put 'em in.   [*They divide raisins.*

BETHIA (*eating them*). This is a good deal better than washing down the back steps at home.

SOPHIA (*eating*). Yes, or weedin' the onion bed. We don't have no raisins at our house.

BETHIA. I guess *not!* When I get married it won't be to a deacon.   [*They eat raisins, only putting one in dish occasionally.*

SOPHIA. What will it be?

BETHIA. Oh, a grocery-man! and I'll have the house chuck full of good stuff to eat. What be you goin' to marry?

SOPHIA. Oh, a man what keeps a store! and I'll have new dresses every day in the week, with long trails to 'em.

BETHIA. Shan't you hold 'em up?

SOPHIA. No! jest trail 'em right through the mud an' dirt, as if they didn't cost a cent. What should I care? The store would be full of 'em!

BETHIA. Pr'aps your husban' wouldn't give 'em to you! Pr'aps he'd run off an' leave you!

SOPHIA. Well, he couldn't take the store.

BETHIA (*eating last raisin in her lap, looks at dish and holds it down*). Here, hand me your dish, an' I'll empty my raisins into it.

SOPHIA (*looking at her dish and holding it down*). No, hand me yours.

BETHIA (*facing her*). Sophia Zeniah Hardscratch, I'll bet you've eat them raisins!   •

SOPHIA. I hain't eat 'em all.

BETHIA. How many you got?

SOPHIA (*looking in dish*). Six; how many have you?

BETHIA (*looking in dish*). Four. (*Facing each other, stare blankly.*) What are we goin' to do?

SOPHIA. Eat the rest of 'em an' say the cat got 'em when we went to wash our hands.

BETHIA. Yes, I guess that's 'bout all we *can* do.   [*They eat raisins and place one dish in other, and set them on floor.*

SOPHIA. I don't like raisins so awful well, do you?

BETHIA. No, they're kind of sickish.

SOPHIA (*wiping hands on apron*). My hands ain't very sticky, are yours?

BETHIA (*putting fingers in mouth and wiping them on apron*). Not so very.

SOPHIA. Let's not wash. (*Taking up skirt.*) That's an awful pretty skirt, ain't it? I'm goin' to have one jest like it when I marries the man what keeps store. (*Putting skirt on.*) Play I lived here and you was my hired girl.

BETHIA. I ain't a goin' to be no hired girl!

SOPHIA. Oh, jest for a few minutes, then you can dress up. (*Walks up and down, looking at train.*) You go out there (*nods left*) and I'll ring for you.

BETHIA. What if them girls should come?

SOPHIA. Oh, we'll watch for 'em.

[BETHIA *goes to door* L. SOPHIA *rings bell, at table* R., *and* BETHIA *comes down stage.*

SOPHIA. Bridget Ann Burke, you don't earn your salt.

BETHIA. Please, marm, I don't eat salt.

SOPHIA. Have you mowed the lawn?

BETHIA. Yes, marm.

SOPHIA. And milked the ten cows?

BETHIA. Yes, marm.

SOPHIA. And scoured my di'mond ring?

BETHIA. Yes, marm, an' I'm awful tired.

SOPHIA. Well, you may rest while you tie my shoe. (BETHIA *stoops and ties her shoe.*) Bridget Ann Burke, who was that man I saw in the kitchen last night?

BETHIA. He was my first cousin.

SOPHIA. What was he doin' here?

BETHIA. Nothin', marm.

SOPHIA. He was! He was eatin' pie. I saw him with both of my eyes. I hid that piece of pie for my brekfus', an' you let him have it. You can't work for me no more.

BETHIA (*kneeling and clinging to skirt*). Oh, please, marm, don't turn me off! I've got ten brothers an' eight sisters a-starvin'!

SOPHIA. Rise up on to your feet. There is a half a loaf of bread in the buttery; give it to 'em an' never show your face here no more! Stop your weepin', an' hand me that hat! (*Points to hat on couch.*) I'm a-goin' to the circus.

[BETHIA *gives her hat ; she puts it on, and walks up stage.*

BETHIA. Let me go, too, marm! I want to see the snake-charmer. She is my sister.

SOPHIA. Bridget Ann Burke, never speak to me no more! I do not 'sociate with snake-charmers' sisters!

Enter ELINOR, BERNICE, LAURA *and* CLARICE C., *they start in astonishment.*

BERNICE. Why, Sophia! what does this mean? Why did you put that skirt on?

BETHIA. I—I—jest had her slip it on to see where we had better begin to rip.

ELINOR. Oh, Bethia!

CLARICE. Where were you going with my hat, Sophia?

SOPHIA. I—I put it on 'cause my head was cold.

. . [*Girls laugh.*

ELINOR. Take those things off at once, Sophia.

[*She takes them off.* BETHIA *assisting her.*

LAURA (*discovering empty dishes*). Where are the raisins, girls?

BETHIA. Ain't they there? The cat must have eat 'em.

BERNICE. Oh, girls, girls, I am afraid you did not go to Sunday-school last week.

SOPHIA. Yes, we did, and mother made us learn twenty-seven verses in the Bible.

LAURA. Poor little imps! don't scold them.

ELINOR. You haven't been good girls and I'm very sorry.

BETHIA. So be we.

SOPHIA. Awful sorry!

BETHIA. Miss Elinor, you won't tell ma we were—were bad, will you?

ELINOR. What would she do?

BETHIA. Lick us like everything.

SOPHIA. Oh, like *everything!*

BERNICE (*to* ELINOR). Life can't be very jolly for them. No, girls, we won't tell that you have been naughty this time, if you'll never do so any more.

BETHIA. We won't, honest and true!

SOPHIA. Hope to die, if we do.

BERNICE. Well, here are some pennies for you. (*Gives them money.*) You can buy some candy and then go home.

BETHIA. You're awful good!

SOPHIA. Yes, you be! [*Exeunt* BETHIA *and* SOPHIA, C.

ELINOR (*laughing*). That's the way Bernice punishes them for being naughty.

BERNICE. Well, haven't they got Mrs. Hardscratch for a mother? and isn't that punishment enough? Why the sight of that woman —— [*Knock heard.*

ELINOR. Hush! some one is at the door. Come in!

Enter MEHITIBLE DOOLITTLE, L.

MEHITIBLE. Oh, you're here, be you? I couldn't find any one in the kitchen.

ELINOR. Good-morning, Miss Doolittle. Come in.

BERNICE. You are quite a stranger.

CLARICE. Yes ; we were speaking of you yesterday.

LAURA. Where have you kept yourself ?

MEHITIBLE. Well, I've been middlin' busy. (*Sits* L.) I've been tackin' comfortables, cannin' plums, an' gettin' ready gen-erally.   [BERNICE *and* LAURA *on couch.*

BERNICE. Oh, yes, for the wedding. When is it ?

MEHITIBLE. In jest two weeks.

ELINOR. Two weeks ! and then you'll be an elder's wife.
                                        [*Sits* R.

MEHITIBLE. Yes ; it's quite an undertakin'.

LAURA. Has he been married more than once before ?

MEHITIBLE. La, yes, three times.

CLARICE (*sits* L. *of table*). Then *he's* used to "under-takin'."

MEHITIBLE. He's always a referrin' to the way Almiry, Dorcas or Phœbe did this, or that. I intend to cure him of such talk as that. He was showin' me over the house one day, and I saw a closet chuck full of dresses, sacks, bunnits, an' sich. "For the land sake !" says I, "whose be these ?" "Them belonged to the dear departed. I've left six hooks, for I shall never marry but once more," says he, smilin' kinder pityin' like at me. "Wall," says I, "you never cared much for dress, an' I reckon those six hooks'll be enough for your clothes." He looked awful queer.   [*Girls laugh.*

CLARICE. I can imagine he would.

MEHITIBLE. Which one of you girls was it that took the twins' picture ?

BERNICE. I am accountable for that, Miss Doolittle.

MEHITIBLE. They beat all I ever see ! Jest as nat'ral as life.

BERNICE. We thought they finished very well.

MEHITIBLE. They did, for a fact ! an' I've been tryin' to get time, for two or three days, to run down an' ask you if you wouldn't take mine.

BERNICE. Take your picture, Miss Doolittle ? Why I should be delighted. Just let me get my camera.   [*Exit* C.

MEHITIBLE! I'm afraid it's makin' an awful lot of trouble.

LAURA. Trouble ! Why nothing pleases Bernice so much as to have a new subject. She has taken everything about the place, even to the pigs and hens.

Re-enter BERNICE, C., *with camera.*

BERNICE. Here we are, Miss Doolittle !

MEHITIBLE. Wall I was thinkin' I'd like one for the elder.

ELINOR. I am sure he would prize it.

MEHITIBLE. And I want it to be a little out of the ordinary run of pictures.

BERNICE (*puzzled*). A little out of the ordinary run ?

MEHITIBLE. Yes ; I want it to mean something. You see I won the elder's heart with my catarrh snuff ; so I thought it would be ruther 'propriate to have it took with a box in my hand !

BERNICE (*laughing*). Oh, I understand ! a symbolical picture.

MEHITIBLE. Yes, diabolical, that's it !

BERNICE. Now stand right here, please. [*Places her* C.

MEHITIBLE (*taking box from pocket*). There,' how's this ? I'll jest hold the box so, and the other hand over my heart, so.
[*Takes position indicated.*

BERNICE. Capital !   [*Girls laugh, aside.*

CLARICE. Yes, that is very artistic.

ELINOR. How pleased the elder will be !

MEHITIBLE (*still posing*). Yes, he'll laugh nigh out loud when he sees it, he'll be so tickled.

BERNICE. Now stand perfectly quiet.

MEHITIBLE. Wait till I swaller. I s'pose I mustn't wink.
[*Stares vacantly.*

BERNICE. There ! I expect that will be the best picture I've taken yet !   [MEHITIBLE *has not moved.*

CLARICE. It cannot fail to be.

BERNICE. That's all, Miss Doolittle. The picture is taken.

MEHITIBLE. Want to know ! Quick work, hain't it.

BERNICE. Yes, rather. The elder won't have to wait long before he shall have his picture.   [*Exit* C.

MEHITIBLE. I mean to frame it in green moss before I send it. I don't intend to let Samanthy know nothin' about it. She'd think 'twas awful silly ; but she was kinder frisky, herself, before she caught the deacon. I remember when she was courtin' him, she made him let his hair grow, so's she could have a bracelet made out of it. His hair never was so awful thick, so she used part horse-hair.

CLARICE (*laughing*). People who are in love will do strange things. Girls will be girls, you know. ·

MEHITIBLE (*giggling*). Yes, we all must have our day. (*Re-enter* BERNICE, C.) I'm awful obleeged to you.

BERNICE. Don't mention it ; you are very welcome.

MEHITIBLE. Wall, I must hurry home 'cause I've got to string some beans for dinner. When's Miss Dexter comin' home ?

ELINOR. She did not tell us just when, but I expect her any day.

MEHITIBLE. Started rather suddint, didn't she.

ELINOR. Rather.

MEHITIBLE. Wall, that's the way to have the best time ; jest start right off, without tirin' yourself out gittin' ready. (*Going.*) Good-bye all.

GIRLS. Good-bye, Miss Doolittle !

ELINOR. Come again. [*Exit* MEHITIBLE, L.

BERNICE. What *will* the elder say when he sees that picture ?

CLARICE. He won't say anything ; he'll be struck dumb.

ASHRAEL (*outside*). Yes, 'tis awful hot walkin' in the sun.

BERNICE. Here's Ashrael at last.

Enter ASHRAEL, *with bag.*

ASHRAEL. There ! I b'leeve I hain't forgot nothin'. (*Takes packages from bag and puts them on table,* R.) There's the salted almonds for you, Miss Elinor.

ELINOR. How good of you to remember, Bernice.

ASHRAEL. And a box of candy for you, Miss Clarice.

CLARICE. Oh, Bernice !

ASHRAEL. Writin' paper, two yards blue ribbon, four yards of lace, three spools of silk, and a crochet-hook for you, Miss Bernice. (*Wiping face.*) Whew ! it's awful hot !

BERNICE. You were a long time, Ashrael.

ASHRAEL. Yes, I was detained a little. Guess who I saw ?

ELINOR. The twins.

ASHRAEL. Twins ? no ! One of a kind will do for me. (*To* BERNICE.) Can't you guess ?

BERNICE. I've no idea.

ASHRAEL. Give it up, hey ? Well, I saw Billy Griffin, a-lias, the runaway lover.

GIRLS. No !

ASHRAEL. Yes, I did, as true as I live ! and I gave him a lesson he won't forget in a hurry.

ELINOR. What did you do, Ashrael ?

ASHRAEL. I was just comin' out of Rogerses store when I met him face to face.

BERNICE. Did he speak ?

ELINOR. How did he look ?

ASHREAL. Turrible ! just as if he'd had a fit of sickness. I purtended not to see him, but he walked right up an' said ! " Oh, Ashrael, how could I ever have done it !" "Sir ?" said I with an awful vacant stare. "Oh, Ashrael !" he says agin, "she's a reg'lar fiend, an' I wish I was dead forty times a day ! I'd rather have your little finger, than——" " My good man," says I, " you must be insane. I have never sot eyes on you before !" [*Girls laugh.*

CLARICE. Oh, Ashrael !

ELINOR. Did you say that ?

ASHRAEL. I jest did ! an' he ketched hold of my sleeve, an' says : " You don't know me, Ashrael ? Ah this is more crueller than death !" Jest then a perliceman came along an' I says : "Mister Perlice, here's a man what's crazy as a loon. I was just makin' a few purchases, pre'vus to goin' to Paris, an' he insists on molestin' me. I wish you'd take him in charge." An' he hooked on to Billy's arm in spite of him a tryin' to explain, an' the last thing I seen, he was a yankin' him down the street.

[*Girls laugh.*

BERNICE. Served him right, Ashrael.

LAURA. " Hell hath no fury like a woman scorned ! "

ASHRAEL (*shocked, aside to* BERNICE). Land sake ! does she swear ?

BERNICE (*laughing*). Oh, no. That was a quotation, Ashrael.

ASHRAEL. Well, it sounded to me like swearin'.

ELINOR. You are well rid of that fellow, Ashrael.

ASHRAEL. I reckon I know it. Well, I'll just run upstairs an' slick up your room, Miss Bernice, an' then, if there's anything to do, I'll be ready for it.

BERNICE. Come, Laura, we'll go with you. There are ever so many things to do.

ASHRAEL. Well, I'm just the girl to tackle 'em !

[*Exit* BERNICE, LAURA *and* ASHRAEL, C.

ELINOR. How glad I am Ashrael is so happy ! She is a rough diamond, but the worth is there, and polishing will show what she really is. Now I'm going into the garden to pick some currants, and if Aunt Debby doesn't come home right away I'll try my hand at currant jelly.

CLARICE. I'll go with you.

ELINOR. No, the sun is hot and your head will ache. Just keep cool, my dear, that's my advice. [*Exit* L.

CLARICE. May be she is right. The sun plays havoc with my weak head. (*Drops into chair* R.) Dear me, I haven't the strength of a mouse. I'm indigo all of the time and it's a perfect force trying to be jolly for, as Lowell says : " When I'm smiley 'round the mouth, I'm teary 'round the lashes." Heigho ! I'd never have believed, two years ago, that any man could have given me such a heartache. Maybe it's Edith's engagement that makes my own trouble seem harder. Dear little girl, how happy she is ! I hope nothing will ever happen to destroy her trust. [*Leans head on hand.*

Enter EDITH *with letter in hand*, C.

EDITH. Oh, I'm so out of breath and my head is spinning round like a top ! I must find Clare at once. (*Discovers her.*)

Oh, there you are ! Clarice Fenleigh, I was never so happy in my life ! I could scream, dance, run !

CLARICE (*rising*). What in the world is the matter, Edith !

EDITH. Lots ! Oh, dear, let me get these gloves off and sit down and gather my wits, like a rational being.

[*Removes hat and gloves.*

CLARICE. Sit here, dear, and get cool. (*She sits L. of table R.*) Here is a fan. (*Gives fan.*) You have been rather flighty for several weeks, but I've never seen you quite as bad as this. What is it ? (*Sits R. of table.*) Has some wonderful good fortune befallen Dick ?

EDITH. Oh, he's the dearest, best boy in all the world !

CLARICE. No doubt of it, I shall offer no argument.

[*Laughs.*

EDITH. And I would hug him, if he were here.

CLARICE. Oh !

EDITH. And so would you.

CLARICE. No, I wouldn't.

EDITH. Then you'd be an ungrateful little minx ! Oh, I was positive he'd do it ! but I didn't say a word. Do you see that letter, miss ? [*Holding up letter.*

CLARICE. I see an envelope ; cream color, ordinary size, nothing extraordinary to look at.

EDITH. You just wait ! That letter will make you so happy you won't know where you're at ! That letter is from Dick.

CLARICE. How can it interest me ? Edith, I thought you had left off using slang.

EDITH. I don't care a rap about slang ! Oh, dear, where shall I begin !

CLARICE (*laughing*). Begin at the end.

EDITH. Good idea ! Well, then, Miss Clarice Fenleigh, you will be engaged to Charles Grierson, Jr., this very night.

CLARICE (*rising*). Edith !

EDITH. There, there, sit down and get ready to be happy. (CLARICE *sits.*) Well, you know that day I went driving with Dick ?

CLARICE. Yes.

EDITH. Well, I asked him if he knew where Charlie was, and he said he left him in the Adirondacks ; that he tried to have him come up here with him, but he refused when he learned you were here.

CLARICE (*bitterly*). Naturally.

EDITH. Well, then, I just told Dick every word that you told me.

CLARICE. Oh, Edith ! I'll never forgive——

EDITH. Yes, you will, and thank me, too ! Well, Dick said, as I did, that there was some mistake.

CLARICE. I don't believe it.

EDITH. Well, you'll have to ! So Dick went straight back to the Adlrondacks the very next day. Charlie had gone from there, and he's been following him from place to place, until he located him a week ago, and this is what Dick says.

[*Takes letter from envelope.*

CLARICE. Oh, Edith, go on !

EDITH. Getting a little nervous yourself, aren't you, Miss Placidity ? Well, I shan't read you how it begins, but just what concerns you.

CLARICE. Yes, yes.

EDITH (*reading letter*). "Found Grierson to-day, after chasing him all over the country.' He's more deeply in love than any man you ever saw, except one——" Oh, dear, I didn't mean to read that, " and that bouquet business caused all the trouble. You see it was like this. Charlie went to the florist's and ordered two boxes of flowers ; English violets for his sister, who was ill, and roses for Miss Fenleigh. The mistake was, of course, made in delivering the boxes. I've just explained matters and I never saw a happier fellow in my life. We leave here to-day and shall be with you Thursday evening." That's to-night. "Don't say a word ; Grierson has the ring in his pocket and it's a sparkler !" There, I'm not going to read another line. Why don't you speak ?

CLARICE (*rises and walks* L.). I am so dazed, dear, that I'm afraid to speak, afraid to tell you how happy I am, for fear it is not real.

EDITH. Well, I reckon, you'll find it's real when you see him. I think it's the jolliest thing I ever knew.

CLARICE (*arm about* EDITH). And you did all this for me ! Sent your sweetheart away, when you would have been so happy to have him near you, and ——

EDITH. If he hadn't gone I should never have cared one bit for him, never !

Enter ASHRAEL C., *out of breath.*

ASHRAEL. Miss Dexter's come ! The stage is at the door ! Where's Miss Elinor ?

[*Exit* L., *calling,* "*Miss Elinor ! Miss Elinor !*"

Enter AUNT DEBBY, BERNICE *and* LAURA C., BERNICE *carrying satchel, wraps, etc.,* LAURA *box and umbrella. Girls surround her.*

EDITH. Oh, Aunt Debby, you've come !   [*Kisses her.*

CLARICE. And I'm so glad. Do stand back, Edith, and let me have a chance !   [*Kisses her.*

LAURA.   Sit right down here and let us take your things off.
[*They seat her at table* L., *and remove her bonnet,
gloves, etc.*
AUNT DEBBY.   Be careful of that box, Laura, my dear.
LAURA.   I've put it over on the table there, Aunt Debby.
AUNT DEBBY.   How good you all are !   But where's Elinor ?
[ELINOR *and* ASHRAEL *running on* L.
ELINOR.   Here I am !   (*Embracing her.*)   I was in the
garden and I fairly flew to get here.   You don't know how I've
missed you.   Ashraèl, bring a glass of wine.   Aunt Debby looks
tired.   (ASHRAEL *going.*)   I say, Ashrael !   (*Aside to her.*)
Do not tell Aunt Debby that Bridget and Jane are gone.   Wait
until she rests a little.   (*To* CLARICE.)   Tell the girls not to
mention it.
[*Exit* ASHRAEL L.; CLARICE *whispers aside to* EDITH,
BERNICE *and* LAURA.
AUNT DEBBY.   I am a little tired.   Travelling is new busi-
ness for me.   How good it was of you girls to wait for my
return !   I'm afraid it has been a sad inconvenience.
BERNICE.   Laura and I could stay as well as not, and I'm
pretty sure Edith and Clarice aren't in any great rush to get
back to "Finikins."
EDITH (*mysteriously*).   I'm not so sure we shall go back.
BERNICE.   What do you mean ?
EDITH.   Just stand back, while I whisper to Aunt Debby.
[*Pushing girls aside, whispers to* AUNT DEBBY.
LAURA.   Well, I like *that!*   What's up, Clarice ?
CLARICE.   I—I am sure—I——
EDITH.   Don't ask her, but to-night (*mysteriously*) when
the clock strikes twelve, I will a tale unfold——

Enter ASHRAEL L., *with glass of wine.*

ASHRAEL.   This will put some life into you, Miss Dexter.   I
tell you it seems good to see you again, for, somehow, I couldn't
help feelin' that a burglar had broke into the house an' carried
everything out of it.   And now I'm jest goin' to get luncheon
ready for you.
AUNT DEBBY (*drinks wine*).   Tell Bridget——
ASHRAEL.   Oh, never mind Bridget, she's tired ; I can do it
jest as well as she can.
[*Exit* ASHRAEL L., *winking at girls.*
AUNT DEBBY.   It's worth going away to receive such a welcome as this.   My heart was very heavy when I left, but
now, it's lighter than it has been for years.
ELINOR.   Lean back in your chair, Aunt Debby, and don't
try to talk until you get rested.
AUNT DEBBY.   I cannot, my dear.   Why, I could scarcely

wait until I got here, I have so much to tell. No, I cannot rest until I have unburdened my heart. Sit down, my dears. Elinor, sit here at my feet. (BERNICE *and* LAURA *sit at table* R., CLARICE *and* EDITH *on couch*, ELINOR *at* AUNT DEBBY'S *feet.*) I'm not a good hand at telling fairy-tales, but this sounds so much like one that, as the twins say, I've felt like pinching myself to see if it were true.

BERNICE. I know it's something nice, for Aunt Debby looks so happy.

AUNT DEBBY. One summer evening, a long time ago, a lonely old maid found a dear little baby, in a basket, at her door. She took the little one to her heart and home, without knowing her parentage. Eighteen years later, when the baby had grown to be a young woman, and the sunshine of the home into which she had come so strangely, an old gipsy woman died, and confessed to this woman that she had stolen this child from a rich family in St. Louis, because they had driven the gipsies off their land.

ELINOR. Oh, Aunt Debby! [*Rises and stands beside her much agitated.*

AUNT DEBBY. The poor old maid wanted to ascertain if the story was quite true, so she never said a word, but started to find the family the old gipsy had told her of.

BERNICE. Why, Aunt Debby, that was you!

EDITH. And the child was——

LAURA *and* CLARICE. Elinor!

ELINOR (*kneeling by* AUNT DEBBY). Oh, Aunt Debby, go on!

AUNT DEBBY. And so the old maid went to St. Louis and found——

ELINOR. Yes?

AUNT DEBBY. Found the father! (ELINOR *kneels and buries face on* AUNT DEBBY's *shoulder.*) The mother had been dead ten years. (*All rise.*) Yes, my Elinor, your father awaits his child. He had been ill and was not strong enough to come to you, but he is longing for you every hour. You will be very proud of your father, Elinor, for you are the daughter of the Honorable Richard Arlington, whose name is a power where he is known.

ELINOR (*throwing arms about her neck*). Oh, Aunt Debby, I can never leave *you*.

GIRLS. No, indeed!

AUNT DEBBY. The sweetest part of it all to me is that I am to go with my little girl, to stay with her always.

ELINOR. Oh, Aunt Debby, is it true?

BERNICE. Isn't it glorious?

CLARICE. Better than any fairy-tale I ever heard!

EDITH. Let me hug you, Elinor.

4

GIRLS.   Pass her round.

[EDITH *embraces her and turns her once around into*
CLARICE'S *arms, same business with* LAURA *and* BER-
NICE ; *girls all laughing, saying, " My turn next ; pass
her to me." etc.*

AUNT DEBBY (*giving* ELINOR *box*).   Your father sent you
these flowers, Elinor, with his dearest love.

GIRLS.   Aren't they lovely.   [ELINOR *sits at table* R., *gazing
                                     at flowers lovingly.*

LAURA.   Is he rich, Aunt Debby ?   .

AUNT DEBBY.   As the prince in the fairy-tale !

BERNICE.   But, Aunt Debby, what's to become of us ?   We
can't come to Breezy Point again.

AUNT DEBBY.   This will be my summer home and yours, as
long as you wish to make it so.

BERNICE.   Glory !

EDITH.   Three cheers for Aunt Debby !

LAURA.   And Lady Elinor !

CLARICE.   And dear old——

GIRLS.   Breezy Point !

[AUNT DEBBY *back of* ELINOR'S *chair,* R., ELINOR *holds
her hands about her neck, looking up into her face lov-
ingly.   Chair at table left, swung around with back
facing stage centre.   EDITH kneeling in it, facing* CLAR-
ICE, *who holds her hands, one arm about her.* BERNICE
and LAURA *centre.   Pause for tableau ; then a noise of
wheels outside and a loud masculine voice crying
" Whoa, whoa, boy !"* .

ASHRAEL (*running on* C.).   Oh, Miss Bernice, they is two
young men jest drove up in a buggy an' they're comin' in.

[*All rise and turn towards door* C., *forming picture.*

BERNICE.   See who they are, Ashrael.   [*Goes* L.

LAURA (*to* L.).   Yes, hurry, Ashrael.

[CLARICE *and* EDITH *rise and come* C., *looking up stage ;
a pause of suspense, then—*

ASHRAEL (*running in* C., *in a hoarse whisper*).   It's Mr.
Richard Coleman and Mr. Charles Grierson.   (*Looking off ;
aloud.*)   This way, gentlemen.   .

[*General expectancy ; just as the two men are about to enter.*

CURTAIN.

www.ingramcontent.com/pod-product-compliance
Lightning Source LLC
Chambersburg PA
CBHW021234260626
47172CB00002B/760